Praise for
CHRISTMAS EVERY MORNING

"*Christmas Every Morning* is Lisa Bergren's best yet! Strong characters dealing with passionate life-and-death issues in a Southwest setting so authentic I could taste the chilies and smell the sage. A compelling story of longing, love, and the search for life.... It's a story to meet the need in every woman's heart."

—JANE KIRKPATRICK, author of *A Name of Her Own*
and the Kinship and Courage series

"Bergren just keeps getting better. *Christmas Every Morning* is a deeply moving story of love lost and found. It is also a gentle but compelling invitation to remember the things we should know by heart but often forget along the way."

—CAROLYN ARENDS, recording artist and author of
We've Been Waiting for You

"Lisa Bergren writes like a dream, softly calling us to familiar places, walking us through our memories in grandma's kitchen, past the disappointments of growing up, and through the complexities of imperfect families. Do not mistake *Christmas Every Morning* for a holiday romance. It is a timeless tale, to be kept every day in the heart as a reminder that forgiveness is a gift to self and joy the glittering residue left upon our doorpost when Christmas is kept every day of the year."

—PATRICIA HICKMAN, author of *Sandpebbles* and
Katrina's Wings

Praise for
THE BRIDGE

"*The Bridge* is an absorbing human drama complete with romantic undercurrents and spiritual eddies. Written with a deft hand, it will introduce you to people you will want as friends and to a country setting so breathtaking you won't want to leave. This is one of those novels you don't just read, you live it."

—JACK CAVANAUGH, author of *While Mortals Sleep*

"Lisa Tawn Bergren spreads a banquet fit for story lovers in *The Bridge*. This story of hope, honor, and love provides a feast of imagery from the opening scene all the way through. Don't be surprised if you find yourself weeping on the last page even while you smile."

—ROBIN JONES GUNN, author of the Glenbrooke series

"In *The Bridge,* Lisa Tawn Bergren has written a tender story of love—the love between a man and a woman, the love between a father and his son, and the love that God showers upon us all. It's a story that will linger in your heart long after the last page is read."

—ROBIN LEE HATCHER, author of *Ribbon of Years*

"Lisa Tawn Bergren writes incredible stories, and this powerful tale with its unforgettable characters and layers of emotion is her absolute best yet. *The Bridge* will stay with you long after the last page is turned."

—DIANE NOBLE, author of *Heart of Glass*

"Another winner! *The Bridge* is a beautiful story. A must-read for all of Lisa Bergren's avid fans. Once again she has created great characters and a story that will be sure to please everyone. Of all her fine books, *The Bridge* is now my favorite."

—LINDA CHAIKIN, author of the Day to
Remember series

"*The Bridge* grabs your heart and never lets go, sending it rushing downstream toward a heart-wrenching yet ultimately redemptive conclusion. Bergren has outdone herself with this powerful story. Not to be missed!"

—LIZ CURTIS HIGGS, author of *Bad Girls of the Bible*

Christmas
Every Morning

Christmas
Every Morning

Lisa Tawn Bergren

WATERBROOK
PRESS

F
BER

CHRISTMAS EVERY MORNING
PUBLISHED BY WATERBROOK PRESS
2375 Telstar Drive, Suite 160
Colorado Springs, Colorado 80920
A division of Random House, Inc.

The characters and events in this book are fictional, and any resemblance to actual persons or events is coincidental.

ISBN 978-1-57856-271-8

Printed in the United States of America

For Mom,
who has always been what I needed in a mother.
I love you.

Acknowledgments

I must acknowledge that it was my sister-in-law, Cara Berggren, who told me what she had heard about a Christmas room in a remarkable Alzheimer's unit. I took the story from there, but she planted that excellent seed. Without our conversation in the car that day, this tale would never have been told.

Many thanks to Kim Alinder, Debi Brown, and Heidi Endicott, women experienced in dealing with loved ones and patients afflicted with Alzheimer's disease. They checked my manuscript for inconsistencies and shared other ideas with me that would bring the "true" experience home.

Becky Albright, a friend and family counselor, helped me muddle through Krista's issues with Charlotte and make them more believable. And my uncle, Dr. Cecil Leitch, made sure I got the medical stuff right.

Cheryl Crawford, faithful friend and prayer warrioress, helped me through this project with encouragement and kind words and cards, while my editors, the incomparable Erin Healy and Traci DePree, never fail to help me produce the best book I have in me.

If you haven't been to Taos, New Mexico, try to do so. It's an amazing place to visit. Tim and I stayed at a lovely B&B (www.spiritandwind.com) and canvassed the city and environs. Smaller than Santa Fe, more mountainous than desertlike, still artsy. Wonderful!

We are all always beginners.

—THOMAS MERTON

Though outwardly we are wasting away,
yet inwardly we are being renewed day by day.

—2 CORINTHIANS 4:16

PROLOGUE

"She's dying, Krista."

I took a long, slow breath. "She died a long time ago, Dane."

He paused, and I could picture him formulating his next words, something that would move me. Why was my relationship with my mother so important to him? I mean, other than the fact that she was a patient in his care. "There's still time, Kristabelle."

I sighed. Dane knew that his old nickname for me always got to me. "For what? For long, deep conversations?" I winced at the harsh slice of sarcasm in my tone.

"You never know," he said quietly. "An aide found something you should see."

"What?"

"Come. I'll keep it here in my office until you arrive. Consider it a Christmas present."

"It's December ninth."

"Okay, consider it an early present."

It was typical of him to hold out a mysterious hook like that. "I don't know, Dane. The school term isn't over yet. It's a hard time to get someone to cover for me." It wasn't the whole truth. I had an assistant professor who could handle things on her own. And I could get back for finals. Maybe. Unless Dane wasn't overstating the facts.

"Krista. She's *dying*. Her doctor tells me she has a few weeks, tops. Tell your department chair. He'll let you go. This is the end."

I stared out my cottage window to the old pines that covered my yard in shadows. The end. The end had always seemed so far away.

Too far away. In some ways I wanted an end to my relationship with my mother, the mother who had never loved me as I longed to be loved. When she started disappearing, with her went so many of my hopes for what could have been. The road to this place had been long and lonely. Except for Dane. He had always been there, had always waited. I owed it to him to show. "I'll be there on Saturday."

"I'll be here. Come and find me."

"Okay. I teach a Saturday morning class. I can get out of here after lunch and down there by five or six."

"I'll make you dinner."

"Dane, I—"

"Dinner. At seven."

I slowly let my mouth close and paused. I was in no mood to argue with him now. "I'll meet you at Cimarron," I said.

"Great. It will be good to see you, Kristabelle." I closed my eyes, imagining him in his office at Cimarron Care Center. Brushing his too-long hair out of his eyes as he looked through his own window.

"It will be good to see you, too, Dane. Good-bye."

He hung up then without another word, and it left me feeling slightly bereft. I hung on to the telephone receiver as if I could catch one more word, one more breath, one more connection with the man who had stolen my heart at sixteen.

Dane McConnell remained on my mind as I wrapped up things at the college, prepped my assistant, Alissa, to handle my history classes for the following week, and then drove the scenic route down to Taos from Colorado Springs, about a five-hour trip. My old Honda Prelude hugged the roads along the magnificent San Luis Valley. The valley's shoulders were still covered in late spring snow, her belly carpeted in a rich, verdant green. It was here that in 1862 Maggie O'Neil single-handedly led a wagon train to settle a town in western Colorado, and nearby Cecilia Gaines went so crazy one winter they named a waterway in her honor—"Woman Hollering Creek."

I drove too fast but liked the way the speed made my scalp tingle when I rounded a corner and dipped, sending my stomach flying. Dane had never driven too fast. He was methodical in everything he did, quietly moving ever forward. He had done much in his years since grad school, establishing Cimarron and making it a national think tank for those involved in gerontology. After high school we had essentially ceased communication for years before Cimarron came about. Then when Mother finally got to the point in her descent into Alzheimer's that she needed full-time institutionalized care, I gave him a call. I hadn't been able to find a facility that I was satisfied with for more than a year, when a college friend had shown me the magazine article on the opening of Cimarron and its patron saint, Dane McConnell.

"Good looking *and* nice to old people," she had moaned. "Why can't I meet a guy like that?"

"I know him," I said, staring at the black-and-white photograph.

"Get out."

"I do. Or did. We used to be...together."

"What happened?" she asked, her eyes dripping disbelief.

"I'm not sure."

I still wasn't sure. Things between us had simply faded over the years. But when I saw him again, it all seemed to come back. Or at least a part of what we had once had. There always seemed to be a submerged wall between us, something we couldn't quite bridge or blast through. So we had simply gone swimming toward different shores.

Mother's care had brought us back together over the last five years. With the congestive heart failure that was taking her body, I supposed the link between us would finally be severed. I would retreat to Colorado, and he would remain in our beloved Taos, the place of our youth, of our beginnings, of our hearts. And any lingering dream of living happily ever after with Dane McConnell could be buried forever with my unhappy memories of Mother.

I loosened my hands on the wheel, realizing that I was gripping it so hard my knuckles were white. I glanced in the rearview mirror, knowing that my reverie was distracting me from paying attention to the road. It was just that Dane was a hard man to get over. His unique ancestry had gifted him with the looks of a Scottish Highlander and the sultry, earthy ways of the Taos Indians. A curious, inspiring mix that left him with both a leader's stance and a wise man's knowing eyes. Grounded but visionary. A driving force, yet empathetic at the same time. His employees loved working for him. Women routinely fell in love with him.

I didn't know why I could never get my act together so we could finally fall in love and stay in love. He'd certainly done his part. For some reason I'd always sensed that Dane was waiting for me, of all people. Why messed-up, confused me? Yet there he was. I'd found my reluctance easy to blame on my mother. She didn't love me as a mother should, yada-yada, but I'd had enough time with my counselor to know that there are reasons beyond her. Reasons that circle back to myself.

I'd always felt as if I was chasing after parental love, but the longer I chased it, the further it receded from my reach. It left a hole in my heart that I was hard-pressed to fill. God had come close to doing the job. Close. But there was still something there, another blockade I had yet to blast away. I would probably be working on my "issues" my whole life. But as my friend Michaela says, "Everyone's got issues." Supposedly I need to embrace them. I just want them to go away.

"Yeah," I muttered. Dane McConnell was better off without me. Who needed a woman still foundering in her past?

I had to focus on Mother. If this was indeed the end, I needed to wrap things up with her. Find closure. Some measure of peace. Even if she couldn't say the words I longed to hear.

I love you, Krista.

Why was it that she had never been able to force those four words from her lips?

1970

"Silent night, holy night, all is calm, all is bright. 'Round yon virgin, Mother and Child, Holy infant so tender and mild, sleep in heavenly peace; sleep in heavenly peace."

I left my hand on Oma's shoulder as she played the old organ. Opa sang over my shoulder. It felt warm and cozy, singing Christmas carols with my grandparents. All that was missing was my mother's high, clear voice joining in or Elena's warm, lower voice.

I looked around Opa's big belly and spotted Mother sitting beside the living room window. Mother had her fingers on her wedding band, slipping it on and off as she stared outside. She got it when she married my daddy. But I had never seen him. I sighed. I think Mother missed my daddy.

"Come sing with us, Charlotte," Opa said.

She looked over at us, strange-like. Like she had heard Opa speak but didn't hear him, all at the same time. Then she stared outside again. I was sad for her, the way she looked. I don't even think she noticed it was snowing.

Oma started playing the organ again, and later we had a big

dinner, and then the best thing, we opened presents. I hoped that would make Mother happy. She smiled a little and seemed to like the rainbow socks I had got her. But she still looked faraway-like.

When Oma tucked me in that night—we always got to stay at Oma and Opa's on Christmas Eve—I asked her why Mother was acting so sad.

"Your mother is lonely," Oma said, rubbing my cheek.

"Why? She's got us."

"Yes, she does," Oma said, leaning down to kiss me on the forehead. "Sometimes, in the missing of people we don't have, we look right over those we do. We are all very blessed to have you, Krista. I love you, child."

"I love you, too, Oma." I would've told Opa I loved him, too, 'cept he was in his armchair in the living room, already snoring away. And Mother... Well, she said she needed some air after dinner, and she wasn't back yet from her drive.

I had seen Oma and Opa look at each other across the table when she said that, all concerned-like. But they didn't say anything, and I didn't either. I didn't want anything to ruin Christmas.

Chapter One

December 12

On the feast day of Our Lady of Guadalupe—patroness of Mexico and the Americas—as Hispanic Catholics across the Southwest commemorated a vision of the Virgin Mary as an Aztec maiden by playing festive mariachi music, singing *Las mañanitas,* and praying, I pulled off the highway and drove down the long, winding dirt road to Cimarron, situated just north of Taos beneath the great mountain. I braked for a stray dog, maneuvered around washboard ruts from recent rains, and then drove on. Past tiny houses, some with folksy yard art in front—there must have been a thousand wannabe artisans in Taos—others with the native fencing of tiny red cedar saplings carefully woven in a straight line, their tops at varying heights, what I deemed *truly* artistic.

As I crested the last hill, able to see for miles again, I pulled to a stop. I rolled down my window to take in a deep breath of desert sage and the faintest hint of pine. This part of New Mexico was covered with the silver green of sagebrush, and the mountains looked as if they had been steeped in the deep green of pine forest tea, the tops dusted with silver snow. There was sand and red clay, colors of the earth that dominated the range, from taupe to Copper River Salmon to Philippine mahogany. The people who lived here often painted their homes in the same earth tones.

I loved the sensory thrill of the region, the connection between earth and sky and people. It sang to me, as it always had through all my years. God surely wanted his sons and daughters to understand their ties to the land. Had he not formed Adam and Eve of clay? Here it was self-evident. New Mexico's people lived in homes made from the foundations of the earth with roofs made from her bounty. The bright sun awakened people slumbering softly in their beds; warm sunsets brought closure to their days.

Had my mother ever revered the same things I did? By the time I was cognizant, she fancied herself a cousin of the literati that "civilized" Taos, people who loved the unique light and air and history that dominated the New Mexican landscape but irrevocably changed it with their upscale tastes. At one time or another she tried to paint like Georgia O'Keeffe or write like D. H. Lawrence. She wore too much silver-and-turquoise jewelry, inspired as much by the Navajo Indians as the late film star Millicent Rogers. In the end it seemed to me that she had spent her life masquerading as others instead of simply being herself. I never understood her. And she never understood me.

I hungrily scanned the landscape, my eyes settling on the

adobe outside the grounds of Cimarron Care Center, one forever owned by my friend Elena Rodriguez. She was the only friend I ever had that Mother claimed as a friend too. Other than Dane, of course. It had been Elena who had sold the valuable ten acres of land to Dane for his Alzheimer's unit for a fraction of the price it was worth, because she believed in his cause. It was with her I would stay while in Taos; she'd have it no other way. Neither would I.

On the far side of Cimarron I could see another modest adobe home the color of wet sand—Dane's home. In my mind I could see him puttering about his kitchen making soup or sprawled out before a fire in the kiva reading a book. But I knew he was at Cimarron. Dane loved his work and was almost always on site, if not taking care of administration tasks, then simply keeping patients company or walking the halls or grounds.

After a moment I took a deep breath and drove on. Cimarron, situated directly between Elena's and Dane's homes, came into brief view between the hills, then disappeared. What Dane had done with Cimarron's design was ingenious in its ability to safely contain the wandering inhabitants while maintaining a traditional neo-Pueblo style, incorporating the stucco exterior, thick adobe walls, slightly pitched roofline, and rounded corners.

I pulled to a stop outside a huge earthen berm, a man-made hill covered in native desert plants. The rise shielded patients from viewing the cars but not from seeing the outside. Dane had quickly discovered that Alzheimer's patients believed that their ride was arriving to take them home or leaving without them when vehicles were within sight. *When are we going, Krista?* my mother, Charlotte, used to ask me even when we had no place to go. *We're late. You always make me late.*

And there were the times she would take the keys and just drive. It was nothing short of a miracle that she had not killed anyone while on one of her "Sunday drives." Nothing short of miraculous that she herself made it home in one piece. Some things, like driving, it seemed, would always stick in her cloudy brain. Except for her daughter and any semblance of love she had ever carried for her. That had disappeared into the mist.

"Let it go, Krista," I told myself for the thousandth time. Charlotte Mueller had given up trying to love me years before. What made a thirty-seven-year-old still yearn for it? I shook my head. It was nuts. I was here to say good-bye to my mother. Not coax from her some measure of reassurance that I was loved, always had been loved. It was too late for that.

"Dear God," I whispered, "help me let go of it. Help me find my way here."

I reluctantly opened the door of my car and stood groaning at the stiffness in my joints that told of hours on the road. It had been a long time since I had visited. A long time since I had had to face the shell of my mother and the man who now oversaw her care.

I heard a hint of music in the air and started walking toward the south. Taking the winding garden path that rounded the corner, I spied Dane on another berm that, from the top, offered a haunting view of the Sangre de Cristo Mountains. He was lost in his music, and it threatened to draw me in too. I climbed halfway up the hillside but then paused. Dane was a picture worthy of a portrait, sitting on a bench at the top of the slight hill. Behind him the mountains grew Venetian red in the setting sunlight peculiar to this region—truly appearing as "the Blood of Christ"—what the Spanish explorers had named them centuries before. I imagined the explorers seeing them as I was seeing them now, perhaps listening to the very same song Dane played. The snow at the higher elevations grew pink in the sunset light.

The way Dane played his *vihuela,* a half-size version of a twelve-string guitar, was beguiling. Soft in tone, it was perfect for the sad, sixteenth-century Spanish song he was playing, "Romance Antiguo." I closed my eyes, picturing the dance steps that would accompany it and make it complete. He was an accomplished classical guitarist, and to hear him play the old Spanish folk tune was enough to make me pick up my skirts and do a gypsy dance the way my mother taught me as a girl. I would've been tempted, but fortunately I had jeans on.

When he ran his fingers over the last string, extracting the last note, I opened my eyes and pulled my hand to my lips.

He turned to me then, as if sensing my presence, and grinned. "Kristabelle! Had I known you were here, I would've demanded you dance. Only that would have made this evening any more perfect."

I smiled, finding it impossible not to match his grin. "I don't dance much anymore." I wiped my sweaty hands on my jeans, preparing for a professional handshake, not wanting him to find my palms cold and clammy.

He was beside me then, enveloping me in his warm, familiar arms. A friendly hug, not a lover's embrace. "I'm sorry to hear that. When you danced, it was like…you were more alive for the sheer joy of it."

"Yes, well. Life…" I let the rest of my explanation drop. The words in my head sounded empty to me and certainly would to Dane, the man who had it all together. I tried to swallow and cast about for a change in subject. "Place is looking good."

"She is. The plants are maturing, and the walls haven't fallen in yet." He cast me a wry grin. "Come inside. I'll show you what's new." He glanced at me over his shoulder. "It's been awhile."

"It has," I admitted. He offered me a hand down the hillside, but I only smiled and said, "I'm all right."

"Suit yourself." He led the way around to the front entrance. With a swipe of the plastic card that hung from his neck, the door popped open. It was then that I noticed the new wing to Reminiscence Hall. "Is that…Christmas music?" I didn't remember hearing music playing through the hallway speakers the last time I'd visited.

He grinned at me, and I quickly looked away. The man only got better looking with age. Straight teeth, olive skin, and dark blond hair that always drifted into welcoming green eyes that seemed to see through me. "It's December, but it's going to be all Christmas all the time. Year-round. Welcome to our new Christmas room," he said as we entered the large hall, complete with a giant faux evergreen set in the corner and covered in chili pepper lights. The room was decked out for the season. There was even a baby grand piano and a circle of chairs, as if ready for a round of "Joy to the World." There were gift bags full of tissue. "We put small dime-store gifts in them for the residents to unwrap, then we wrap them up again," Dane explained.

There was a miniature crèche set in another corner, complete with a shepherd and a wise man watching over the tiny baby Jesus. Fake candles with steady flames were dancing in each of the three windows. Outside, white Christmas lights hung from the eaves and glowed brightly against a dusky sky. I turned and caught a whiff of cinnamon and nutmeg and pine.

"It's wonderful," I said to Dane.

"I think so. It's been remarkable for your mother."

I shot him a curious look. "How so?"

"This Christmas room is part of the music therapy we do here at Cimarron. Some of the residents who come in here who no longer speak will sing entire Christmas carols from memory."

I shook my head. "Amazing."

"It is. Your mother sang 'Silent Night' by heart. Three whole verses before she stopped."

"*My* mother?"

"Your mother."

I ransacked my memory for when my mother would have last sung the song. We hadn't routinely attended church since I was a kindergartner still content to sit on my grandmother's lap. Mother had been with us at that time but then went on "hiatus from church," as she referred to it, until I was about twelve. We attended on Christmas morning every year with Oma and Opa, when we sang "Joy to the World" but not "Silent Night," and there were never carols in our household after my grandparents died. She didn't allow it, and it was okay with me since the songs reminded me of my loved ones and made me miss them all the more. Even after we started going back to church on occasion, there still wasn't Christmas music in our household come December. That was when her spirits always seemed the lowest. But there were bigger issues on my mind. If she could sing, then... "What does this mean? Does it mean she's...recovering?"

An arrow of sadness flashed across Dane's eyes. "I'm sorry, Krista. You know there's no recovery from Alzheimer's."

"Of course," I said, silently berating myself for my surprising, confusing hope, wondering why I wanted her to recover when I'd been so adamant that I needed to be ready for the end. "It's just that..."

Dane followed me closely with his piercing gaze. "This is just like our other music therapy. They tell me it reaches a different part of a patient's brain, helps explore territory that hasn't been charted and divvied up by the marauding forces of the disease."

I turned away. What was I hoping for? A mother I had always longed for suddenly springing to life, reclaiming our relationship?

"What this does bring is the gift of lost memories. I take it you didn't even know your mother knew the words to three verses of 'Silent Night.'"

"That's true." I paused. I thought I knew everything there was to know about my mother.

"There's more." He led me out of the Christmas room and

down the hall to his office, greeting several patients as we walked. A man I knew as Wally went to lift his hat in greeting but then looked vaguely lost to discover he had no hat on.

"Good afternoon, Alberto," Dane said to a stoop-shouldered Latin man. The gent ignored him and kept walking.

"My kitty's on the roof!" a smallish woman with a tight gray perm said to Dane, a look of fear on her face.

"I'm sorry, Sally," Dane consoled, putting a hand on her forearm. "We'll get someone to fetch her right away." The woman's face relaxed into a smile, and she wandered off.

We stopped to talk with Juan, who seemed very agitated and angry. "That Anita. She doesn't make my bed the way she should," Juan said. "There are no hospital corners. No hospital corners!"

"I will speak to Anita. I am certain that she just forgot."

"See that you do." Seemingly pacified, the silver-haired man went on with his walk, a bit calmer.

"Agreement therapy," Dane explained, moving me onward. "Whatever their complaint, you listen and agree. The aide he's complaining about is nothing short of perfection. But what Mr. Muñoz needs most is to be heard and understood. We can do that for him."

It was one of perhaps ten or more therapies that Dane incorporated into his care of Cimarron's patients. There was an entire hall filled with "Main Street" stores along the way, places in which patients could shop for imitation fruit at the grocer's or get haircuts at the barbershop—often by other patients working with plastic scissors—or find just the right "gift" at the stationery store or flower shop. There were numerous halls with winding path-ways—Alzheimer's patients loved to wander—through indoor gardens and arboretums, past caged birds and planters full of real flowers.

There were four exits locked from the inside and a retired assis-tance dog who was too old to guide people across the street or fetch needed articles but was not too old to bark when a resident needed help or to offer friendly companionship. Often the dog would gen-tly herd them back toward their rooms. It had been Dane's idea to give the dog this "retired career." In return, he got lots of attention, a warm bed by the nurses' station, and plenty of treats. So much so that he was quite overweight.

Dane and I reached the Eisenhower wing, the one farthest from the front entrance. These rooms had peekaboo views of the Sangre de Cristo Mountains. Dane had always taken special care of my mother, including her placement in one of the choicest rooms. He paused at her doorway, letting me go first, giving me room to see Charlotte. My mother sat beside the window in a wheelchair, star-ing outside with blank, watery eyes that were half-opened. Her breath was labored, as if she were inhaling water, as if she needed to cough but lacked the strength. A thin oxygen tube ran from a tank beside her into her nostrils. On a small cassette recorder on the bookshelf, Christmas carols were playing. The only sign of mental activity was the quiet movement of one finger in time with the music.

I sat down on the hard hospital bed beside my mother, who

never looked in our direction, and reached for her hand, which was frail and cold. "Mother, it's Krista. I'm here."

She didn't show any sign that she had heard a thing. She was still apparently lost in the notes of "O Tannenbaum." Dane moved forward then and knelt in front of her. "Hey, old girl. Your daughter just drove all the way down from Colorado. I was telling her you're into Christmas tunes again. May I show her what we found?"

Without waiting for a response, he gently pried Mother's fingers from the weathered blue book in her other hand, *Christmas Carols of the World.* The binding was broken and the cloth covering frayed at the corners. He casually handed it over to me. "After that first day in the Christmas room, when she responded so well, I brought her back to her room. An aide with us spotted that on her shelf."

"She's had it for years," I said, gazing down at the tattered cover. "I never paid much attention to it. One of the many anomalies in my mother's life. A book of carols for a woman I seldom heard sing." I looked over at the small shelf where twenty other old volumes and a collection of coffee table picture books were lodged. "She never even decorated for the holidays."

"Did you ever open the book?"

"No. I guess I became somewhat of a grinch." I could hear the defensiveness in my tone. "Why?"

"Check it out." Dane rose and quickly kissed Charlotte's brow. "Great view of the Sangres today, huh, Charlotte? Don't wear your daughter out with all your gabbing now, you hear me? Share one of your Christmas songs, and that would be enough for one day.

"Give it a chance," Dane encouraged me, studying me a moment too long with those watchful eyes of his.

"I'm here, aren't I?"

"Yes, you are," he said, still lingering as if he wanted to say more. His eyes were alight with the old interest.

I turned away then, wanting to discourage him, and after another glance at the shell that used to be my mother, I opened the book that felt like a hymnal in my hands. Dane slipped out of the room as I began to read. On the first page was an inscription.

December 1932

Our dearest Charlotte,

May you always see the wonder of Jesus' birth in your life,
new every morning.

Mama and Poppa

Oma and Opa. It had been a long time since I had thought about my grandparents, gone twenty-some years. They had been good people, making me wonder about the child they had produced. How had Charlotte been of their blood, their only child?

My eyes fell to the page again. New every morning. That was apropos. Wasn't everything new to Charlotte Mueller now? Every day? I edged away from my own harsh feelings to the words again. How long had it been since I myself had contemplated the wonder of Christmas, new every morning?

I turned the yellowed, thin page. In a childish scrawl, there was more to be read.

December 1932

My name is Charlotte Elizabeth Mueller. I live in Santa Fe, New Mexico. This is the first book I have ever owned. Mama said I could write notes in it from time to time since I do not have a diary like Lillian, and Poppa says we can't afford one. I think I shall write a note come Christmastime. Perhaps it will be more interesting than your average, everyday variety of journals.

I quickly flipped through the book, scanning for more hand-written text and seeing pages of it from time to time, as well as inserted cards and notes. I glanced from the faded script to my mother. It was the most I had heard from the woman in more than five years. No wonder Dane thought it important for me to see.

I took a deep breath and blew out my cheeks. Was I ready to enter? Did I, despite all my whining, really want to know anything more about my mother?

I was still thinking about that when Dane appeared in the doorway. "Ready for dinner? I don't know about you, but I'm starved."

"Listen, I haven't settled in at Elena's. She doesn't even know I'm here yet." Elena had never fully forgiven me for moving away. And it angered her that I had left my mother behind when Charlotte was so needy. But she knew too that I had to have some distance to preserve my sanity.

"So we'll drop by Elena's and say a quick hello, leave your stuff, then take off for dinner."

"Listen, Dane. It's all a bit much. Seeing Mother like this. Coming home at all. Give me a little time, all right?"

"Oh. Sure." I could see the disappointment run across his face as clearly as a storm approaching over the valley floor.

"See you tomorrow?" I offered, hating to hurt him.

"Tomorrow."

"Call me at Elena's if anything changes with Mother, will you?"

"I'll tell the staff."

"Thanks, Dane." I turned then, away from him, and stifled a sigh as I walked down the hall toward the front door. Everything in my heart wanted to go share a meal at some intimate restaurant; everything in my head told me to do anything but that.

I pulled up to Elena's house five minutes later. A mongrel of a dog came out to bark at me but was wagging his tail. Elena had always adopted strays over the years. I stooped to let him sniff my hand, saying softly, "Hey, pooch, what's your name?"

"Samson," Elena said, suddenly on the other side of the fence. "He came by and fell in love with my Delilah. Never strayed again." I swore her method of silent approach was inborn, a gift from her Pueblo Indian ancestors. The Spanish influence was woven in well too, from her father. She was the quintessential *Taoseño*. "I suppose you've forgotten my name; it's been so long since you've visited."

"Uh, yeah. Tell me what it is again?" I cajoled.

Even as she chastised me, the smaller woman pulled me close for a warm embrace. "He called you then about Charlotte."

"Yes," I said, "he did."

"Come inside. You can tell me about her today. I saw her yesterday. She wasn't well."

I obediently followed her past her shop, a small wing of the house just off the kitchen, where she made silver jewelry, wove blankets on a century-old loom, dyed her own yarns, and occasionally tried her hand at ceramics. The scent of corn muffins wafted throughout the house.

She looked well for her seventy-odd years. A little more gray, a little more stiff in her pace, but well. After the sale to Dane of the land for Cimarron, she was financially set. Even though she sold the acreage for a portion of its worth, it had been incredibly valuable, and Dane had wanted to be sure that our adopted "aunt" was taken care of forever. Her own family, other than one son, had moved away long ago to Albuquerque. Not that one would know she was alone. *Doña* Elena always lived life as though she was surrounded by love.

We entered the sitting room to the side. It got the morning sun and was a cheery place to settle. Elena often took her breakfast and entertained guests there. She motioned to a covered wicker chair and immediately poured me a cup of tea from a thermos sitting on the table. She was like that—always ready for a visitor. Then she was gone, presumably to retrieve a batch of fresh-baked corn muffins from the oven.

She had made me feel welcome as a child, never like an intruder. From the first time I met her, when my grandfather took me out to introduce himself and ask if he could run his sheep across her land—in those years when he was still trying to make the ranch work—I had been drawn. She had even accepted my mother, even though I could never comprehend their pairing in my head. Total opposites, they were. Later, in high school, when Dane and I had dated, I had introduced him to her, and he had felt the same way as I. It was just one of many things that Dane and I had shared over the years, this love for Doña Elena.

She returned with a bowl of chicken chili and two muffins. I gratefully accepted them, suddenly ravenous when, at Cimarron, I had thought I wouldn't eat at all that night. I asked her about her arthritis, which I knew bothered her in the winter, and about what she'd sold at the local shops. She asked me about the college, my classes, my students. About my cottage among the old trees of downtown Colorado Springs, which made me suddenly miss its quiet sanctuary. And of course she asked about men. When I shook my head no, responding to whether there were any eligible bachelors in my life, she said, "Still pining for my neighbor then?"

I felt my eyebrows rise in warning. "I just…haven't met anyone."

"That's because you passed up the right one years ago."

"Doña Elena," I said with a sigh.

"All right," she said, holding up her hands in surrender. "I must only speak the truth. Our Lord would accept no less of me. If you felt the same, you'd be agreeing with me, not ducking what is right in front of your face." She raised a basket of more warm muffins to me, as if she had just asked the time of day, not shot an opening salvo at my unprotected chest.

This was the part of Doña Elena that I found less enjoyable—her penchant for saying exactly what she thought. And saying the Lord made her do it. I'd found over the years that if I just said something noncommittal and changed the subject, it was easier than trying to argue with her. But she changed the subject first.

"Eat some butter on that muffin. You are too skinny. Do they not have food in Colorado?"

I laughed and quietly accepted the butter from her. I was ten pounds overweight, but she would always feel the need to feed me and proclaim me "too skinny." Just another of the thousand things that I loved about her.

All in all, it was good to be home.

1972

I skipped home from school singing the song my second grade teacher had taught us for the concert: "Deck the halls with boughs of holly. Fa la la la la, la la la la. 'Tis the season to be jolly. Fa la la la la, la la la la. Don we now our gay apparel. Fa la la, la la la, la la la. Troll the ancient Yuletide carol. Fa la la la la, la la la la."

But as soon as I walked in the door, I could see that Mother was in no mood for yuletide carols. The fa-la-la-la-las faded in my throat as soon as I saw her blue eyes, the same color as mine, narrowed in consternation.

"Where have you been?" she hissed, rising from the kitchen table.

"Nowhere. I just came from school!"

"You're fifteen minutes late! Where were you?"

"I stopped and talked to Lisa Chavez for a minute," I said. She gave me that look that made me want to hide.

"She wanted me to come over and play, but I told her I had to get home." I carefully hung up my coat on the peg and walked down the hallway to my bedroom to place my backpack by my desk.

Mother appeared in my doorway and leaned against the jamb. She *looked upset. I sank down on the bed and waited for her to tell me how I had messed up this time.*

"I'm…I'm sorry, Krista." She lifted a hand to her head. Another headache? Half the time she stayed in bed with "headaches." Shades drawn, dishes in the sink. Oma said it was because she missed my father, a man I'd never met. Opa said she needed to work again, get out.

She walked over to me and ran her long, thin fingers through my hair. "You have his hair, you know."

"Whose?"

"Your father's. He had dark, wavy hair like this." She looked me full in the face. "You have his long, straight nose, his chin. Only your eyes came from me."

I stared back at her. She didn't seem happy that I looked like my father.

She turned and walked away then, pausing at the door. "I'm going to look for him, Krista. I haven't heard from him in a while. I need for him…I have some papers for him."

"Divorce papers?" I'd heard her talking about them with Elena. "Don't divorce him, Mother! If you guys get divorced, I'll never meet him!" All my life all I'd wanted was to meet my father.

Sadness filled her eyes, but she turned and walked away then.

And I was left with the distinct feeling that it was all my fault that my father had left my mother and never came home. Maybe he never wanted a baby. Maybe my mother never wanted me.

I turned and cried into my pillow, stifling my sobs. I didn't want my mother to be sad anymore. But what about me? What about what I wanted?

CHAPTER TWO

December 13

I found the next note on the back of a dance card filled with men's names. It had apparently been my mother's and was stuck in the book of carols. I fingered the smashed, satiny rope that had once encircled a young, happy Charlotte's wrist, took a deep breath, and read her even, loopy script. When she was older, her handwriting had become more angular, less neat. What would a handwriting expert say about that?

Christmas 1937

I have just met the most amazing young man. I attended a holiday ball in Santa Fe with a friend, and we were paired with two gentlemen from the University of New Mexico, both sophomores, studying history. He wanted to attend West Point but hadn't the grades, he said. Now he's bent on proving himself by entering the army as an officer at his first opportunity. I think he'll be most successful. You can see his determination in his piercing green eyes.

His name is Gordon Cooper, and he is ever so handsome. He told me I looked beautiful, and I believe he was telling the truth. I was wearing a new ivory ball gown that Mama said made my blue eyes bluer and my gold hair golder. I felt very grown-up.

Poppa grumbled that he thought Gordon was too old for me, but I could tell when Gordon came to take me out for a soda the next night that Poppa liked him too. He's just five years my senior, and it makes my heart pound to be on the arm of a man—a college man!—and not just another dumb high school boy from Taos.

Oh yes, you don't know this. Poppa moved us to Taos because he said Santa Fe is growing too busy and there was a fierce row over land use rights for those who run sheep or cattle. We now live in a nice adobe right beside the Indian lands near Taos Mountain. I like it here very much. Poppa's running sheep and cattle. Mama bakes her delicious bread to sell at the corner store every Saturday. Enough that she bought me my beautiful ball gown!

I believe that meeting Gordon Cooper two nights past was the most momentous thing that's happened to me in the last five years. This sounds childish, but I think he is the man I'm

*destined to marry. He looks at me with those eyes of his, the color
of deep pools in the Taos River, and I could just stare and stare.
He told me I was the best dancer he'd ever seen, and he's so kind.
When I took his hand in our dance, I thought I never wanted to
let it go. A true gentleman, he is. We'll have to wait a few years,
of course, and he hasn't asked me. But you just wait. Gordon
Cooper will ask me to be his bride someday. And I will be most
happy on his arm forever.*

I looked up at my mother then, searching her features for some
sign of what once was. Some glimpse of youth and hope and love.
We had shared these things. A love of dancing, a love of a man with
green eyes. Her eyes, still only half open but so silver blue, were
swimming in the liquid of old age. Her lids sank to the point that
the pink rims showed. Wrinkles upon wrinkles and sunspots from
too many days in the harsh New Mexico sun for a fair woman of
German descent covered her face and neck until they disappeared
in the soft folds of the Cimarron Care Center–issued bathrobe.
Something had happened along the way to blow out the candle
flame visible in her odd journal's words. Something momentous.
The girl that wrote these words had been full of hope and capable
of the love my grandparents had themselves expressed. What had
doused the flame?

I sighed and shifted uncomfortably. I had spent years merely
tolerating my mother, writing her off as incapable of anything
good. To think that something had happened to cause her to be

that way gave her an excuse, an escape route from my wrath. I didn't like the idea of it—Charlotte Mueller was ultimately responsible, wasn't she? Regardless of what had transpired before?

A nurse appeared and, after checking Mother's vitals, her oxygen tank, and the tube that entered her nose, gave me a brief smile and left us to our silence. I was sure it was a common sight for her, a daughter sitting silently, staring at a vacant mother. How much one-sided conversation could go on?

The level of care here was remarkable. There was an aide for every three residents, two nurses on duty that covered all forty-eight patients, and a doctor who spent two hours on site every day. In addition, Dane had ophthalmologists and hearing specialists and dentists come in regularly. Their brains might be locked up in ever-growing tangles of black neurons, but they would never suffer needlessly or long for anything that Dane McConnell could provide.

It cost a mint to have my mother at CCC. But it eased my guilt for leaving New Mexico, knowing Charlotte was in the best care possible. I had tried to manage her care myself for some time. It had left me exhausted and depressed. In my book Cimarron was worth every penny. Besides, the sale of the family estate had paid for the bulk of Mother's years here. Opa had moved the family to Taos to run sheep, but he had wisely invested his modest savings in property. It was only in the last three months that I had had to pay for her care myself, and soon my mother's congestive heart failure would stop the bills forever.

It sounded cold and callous to be thinking of an end to the exorbitant bills and almost looking forward to it, but I was not alone. There were countless other families who cared for Alz patients, praying that God would take them home, make their loved ones whole again. There was little left for them on earth. They had simply crumbled away. A quote from Aaron Alterra's book *The Caregiver* came to mind: "Everything crumbles, as in movies of rivers in flood, breaking through dikes, overrunning them, inundating the low ground except for random hummocks of refuge, and rising inexorably toward the once-safe house."

Dane ducked in the room then, startling me out of my reverie. "Want to grab some lunch?"

"Oh, thanks. I'm not very hungry."

"Come on. You dodged my dinner invitation—quite artfully by the way…"

"Well, thank you. I try," I said, smiling.

"But not today. Come with me, Kristabelle. It's been too long since we've had a chance to catch up. Your mother needs her rest. I have an aide coming to put her to bed for a while anyway."

"And just when we were getting to some good, meaningful conversation." My stomach rumbled. "A burrito at the Golden Apple would be good."

"Sounds good to me, too. If we hurry, we can beat the lunch crowd and get a table in the courtyard. It's a nice day. I think we'll be warm enough."

"All right."

"You read many of her notes?" Dane asked, holding the side door open for me. We walked out to his old BMW convertible sitting in the employee parking lot.

"Just a couple of entries. Have you?"

"Enough to see that they were meant for you to read. I felt like I was intruding."

"Mother doesn't care."

Dane frowned. He disliked it when people talked about his residents as if they were gone already. His whole life was focused on reaching what was left, what was reachable. He could joke about some things but never about what they were still capable of. Like caring. Yet I doubted my mother had ever cared much about anything but herself. I'd seen too much evidence to the contrary to believe one journal entry.

"Have you seen how the entries are situated throughout the book?" he asked, shutting my door and coming around.

"Yeah." But my mind was drifting to him. I had to admit that it felt good to be looked after by Dane McConnell again. As we drove out, I glanced over to Cimarron and saw several women staring out the window after us. One, a slim brunette in white that I hadn't met yet, looked plainly ticked.

It suited my mood to irritate others. I was all wound up inside, agitated, frustrated, itching for an argument. Taking a deep breath and searching my soul for a measure of control, I asked him, "Why do you think she chose to write in a Christmas carol book of all things?"

"Why do you think your grandparents gave her the book?"

He had seen the inscription too then. "Suits my mother, to find some unique place to journal," I said.

"She said they couldn't afford a real one. I think it was resourceful of her, somewhat artistic."

"Uh-huh," I said noncommittally. I disliked thinking of my mother as resourceful or artistic, regardless of the fact that it had been Charlotte who had once run her own hard-won dance studio. By the time I came along, it had become a storage unit. She cleared it out to teach me and later a few others. It had been the one thing we had ever shared. But those ties had long been severed.

We drove the short distance into town in companionable silence and found a parking spot on the curb beside the Moby Dickens Bookstore, which was across the street from the restaurant. The tall Hispanic man at the front desk of the Golden Apple greeted Dane like an old friend, although he had to be somewhat new to town since I didn't know him. But there were tons of new people in town now. Vacationers, wannabe New Mexicans. Taos had been officially discovered.

The host showed us to a corner table in the courtyard of the old house surrounded by thick, rounded adobe walls painted a rustic brick brown. An old live oak tree lent some shade with its gnarled branches, but the green umbrellas remained furled to allow the warm winter sun to ward off any hint of coolness in the air.

It was a perfect, temperate winter day, the kind of day that made one want to dig out shorts and a long-sleeved T-shirt, well aware that it might be snowing again by moonrise. Both Dane and I opted for the Santa Fe special—a chicken, red pepper, and black bean burrito. We grinned across the table at each other.

"It's been a long time, Kristabelle."

"It has. And would you quit calling me that?"

"Why?"

"It's embarrassing. A teenager's nickname."

"I like it. It fits you."

"Hardly. It's too light. Happy."

"Life's been rough in Colorado Springs, huh?"

"No. I'm just…getting older. Ready for something more solid, a mantle of respectability. Even Krista seems too frivolous."

Dane sat back in his chair and crossed his arms, perusing me. "My, you've gotten awfully tough."

"I'm thirty-seven, looking at forty coming down the road fairly fast; the college is thinking about cutting back the history program; my mother is dying. I'd say that's pretty serious stuff, wouldn't you?"

"Age is a state of mind, I've found. I'm sure there are other colleges that would be happy to get an instructor of your caliber. Every one in New Mexico, for sure, you being a native daughter and all. UNM's been after you for years, right?"

He took a sip of water. "And your mother's death has been coming for a long time. Just think—she'll be released into heaven whole again."

"Assuming she's going to heaven."

He gave me a long look. "Of course. Assuming."

I returned his penetrating gaze. "You always were able to see the silver lining in every storm cloud."

"And you could always make a spring rain a full-blown thunderstorm."

"This is tough stuff, Dane."

"I understand that," he said, his expression sincere, too kind. "Life is tough business. If you don't look for those silver linings, don't you always find yourself drenched from the rain instead of pleasantly cooled off?"

I let a slow smile spread across my face. "So you're saying I'm kinda like Pig Pen with his dust cloud that followed him everywhere?"

Dane smiled too. "Man, you're gorgeous when you smile."

I let the compliment pass without acknowledging it, only let it seep into my lonely heart and warm it. "I guess I need more people in my life to make me smile."

"What? Krista Mueller admitting to a need?"

I fought the urge to squirm and instead crossed my arms. "I'm not that dysfunctional. I've sorted a lot out over the years."

"We're all dysfunctional, Krista, at some level. I've found the key is to move on with what you've been given rather than wallowing in the past."

"Ouch. Come on, Dane, don't pull any punches. Let's just get right to the heart of it. I've been with you, what? A half-hour?"

He didn't blink. "Isn't it imperative that you deal with your issues with your mother now? While you can still speak to her even if she can't talk back? Even if she can't tell you what you want to hear?"

"What do I want to hear?" I asked, trying to buy myself some time.

"What you've always wanted to hear. 'You're good enough,

Krista. You're loved. Please forgive me.' Right? You said it yourself. You're almost forty. It's time to put these issues with your mother to bed, once and for all."

"I don't really want to talk about—"

"We have to talk about it. Over the last five years I've seen your mom every day. You've come, what? Three times total?"

"I've been busy. Setting up new curriculum, research—"

"*Three* times, Krista. In *five* years."

I could feel the slow blush move up my neck as my heart raced. Coolly I folded my cloth napkin and set it beside my unused utensils. "You have no idea what life with my mother was like. No idea. Your life was perfect. Perfect, loving parents. Perfect little sister. Perfect life. You have *no idea* what my life was like." I shoved back my chair and stood up.

"Krista, sit down."

"I'll catch a ride back to Cimarron. I didn't join you for lunch so you could lecture me."

"Krista, wait. *Krista.*"

I maneuvered through the groups of people entering and exiting the restaurant, my fury growing. How dare he! Invite me out for lunch to "catch up" and then subject me to his diatribe! It had always been our problem, his propensity to tell me how to fix my life. I had been a fool to accept his invitation.

The restaurant host gave me a look of curiosity but then lowered his gaze as I bustled past. I could feel his eyes on my back and found some satisfaction in knowing that others had seen me leave Dane McConnell's table. He didn't hold any power over Krista

Mueller, no way. I could agree to his company or leave his side whenever I pleased. Probably one of the few women in Taos capable of doing so, I thought with some satisfaction. No, Dane was not perfect. Despite how he looked and all he had accomplished, there was a lot he didn't do right.

I didn't go back to Cimarron right away, knowing that Dane would look for me there first. Instead, I ducked through the bookstore and walked along a small shopping plaza, entering a quiet alley that led to the main drag of Taos, Paseo del Pueblo Norte. From there, I called a cab with my cell phone and quietly awaited its arrival from the safety of a shop's shadowed window. When the cab arrived, I got in, leaned forward, and said, "Santiago Storage, please."

The cab quickly pulled out into the flow of traffic and headed south, then east. We passed a familiar Hispanic cemetery, each grave site covered in brightly colored plastic flowers from headstone to toe, each one attempting to outdo the others. The effect was always jarring to me, not soothing, the astro-bright pinks and yellows incongruous with the soft-hued Southwestern landscape. I pictured the old cemetery on the hill where Mother had purchased a grave site because "famous people" were buried there. What would I put on her headstone? Just her name and the dates of her birth and death?

It seemed tragic to me. Would I die like her, with no one to write something decent about me on my headstone? Charlotte deserved at least that. I'd come up with something respectful. I could do that. *I better start thinking about it now.* It would take some time.

The cabby pulled up outside of the storage unit where the remains of Mother's belongings were kept. "Want me to come back for you, Toots?"

"I'll call you," I said, taking his proffered card and stuffing it in my pocket. I got out of the beat-up Chevrolet and leaned in to hand him some cash. "You'll be around?"

"Somewhere around town," he said. "Just give headquarters a ring."

I smiled. No one had called me Toots since my Opa died. God had a funny sense of humor. He was always reminding me of things from my past at odd moments. Like now, when I most needed them. Sweet memories of Opa when I was about to dive into sad memories of my mother.

I walked into the main office. The man behind the counter barely lowered his newspaper. "Hi," I said, "I'm the woman who pays the bills for 6E." I waved the key in the air, as if needing to prove it. He nodded backward in a gesture of clearance, and I walked through the gate as it buzzed, feeling as if I were entering a prison.

The ten-by-ten unit was just around the corner, and before I could second-guess the wisdom of this move, I slipped the key into the rusting safety lock and quickly pulled it off. The rolling garage door went up with a pull and a squeaking groan.

For a long moment I just stood and stared, lost in the memories that the dusty furniture and boxes I'd packed years before sent me to. It took some digging, but I eventually found the small box on top of an old dressing table that had once belonged to Oma.

I pulled out a matching wooden chair, brushed off a solid layer of dust, and then sat down, right there in the cement roadway between storage units. Then, taking a deep breath, I opened the Christmas crate and gazed inside.

It was little wonder that I didn't remember many Christmas decorations. There were few to be had. What there was brought back pleasant memories of Oma and Opa's house. Hand-carved little figurines of Saint Nick. A three-level crèche that moved in separate circles when candles were lit beneath the windmill at the top, sending Mary, Joseph, the baby Jesus, animals, and angels on a trek, above two levels of shepherds and sheep and wise men on a permanent pilgrimage. The family Bible was in there, interestingly enough, and I set it to the side of the table to look at later, along with a set of hand-blown German glass ornaments.

There were three Limoges boxes that looked like pretty Christmas packages. I remembered Opa used to give them to Oma every once in a while. Where were the rest of them? Probably spirited off by one of the many home-care workers that I had hired to watch over Mother in the early years, I mused. Many things went missing in that second decade of her downward slide, besides Mother's memories. In 1980 Charlotte began losing words and names. By 1985 she had to have full-time care at home while I attended college classes. Left alone, she took to driving across the country, and it required the police to track her down. In 1990 I sold the house. It was then that I packed up all her belongings and put them in storage. *Like Mother. Neatly squirreled away to deal with at some later date.* I left for Colorado when I could no longer take the pressure of caring for her. I needed out, wanted out.

The guilt had gotten to me eventually, and I moved Mother to several other facilities, one after another. It seemed every other year I would spend the holidays setting things up with a new caregiver. At first it was an in-home situation with six other residents. Then it was a top-rated facility in Santa Fe where, I discovered, they sedated residents to keep them in line. I eventually moved Mother back to a nursing home in Taos, thinking that being in the town of her youth might bring her some measure of comfort. But that didn't work out so well either. Too many times I found Mother restrained in her bed, left in the dark. As much as I understood how hard it was to watch over her, I couldn't allow Charlotte to suffer like that. It was only when Dane opened Cimarron that I found rest. She was in a place of peace, of total care, for the first time in years. They watched over her, provided for her there better than I could.

Three times in five years. He was right. I hadn't come home often enough after she entered Cimarron. By then she was pretty much gone. I hadn't felt the need. Mother certainly couldn't care.

I heard a car entering through the gates and looked over my shoulder. Dane.

I went back to my rummaging, taking out moth-eaten Christmas stockings and a Santa hat that looked as though it had been made in the '20s. Dane's car door slammed as I pulled out the one remaining item—a bundle of cards tied up with a pink satin ribbon.

"They'll let anybody in here, I guess," I said to him over my shoulder, still studying the greeting cards.

"Yeah," Dane said.

He'd probably gone back to Cimarron and Elena's looking for me, then guessed I was here, digging through more of Mother's past. I could sense him nervously shuffling a bit. But still I ignored him, untying the cards and sifting through them. Many were pieces of mail postmarked from around the world. And there were more notes from my mother—on the backs of choir concert bulletins, the edges of class notes, the blank side of Christmas cards. "She was unconventional, my mother," I said in a low tone. "Couldn't even write in a regular journal like everyone else."

"Maybe she was thrifty."

I laughed under my breath. "She'd spend three hundred dollars on a piece of jewelry and then make us eat Hamburger Helper—without meat—for a month. I suppose you could call her thrifty."

"Krista—" He crouched down and placed a hand on my knee.

I stood abruptly and began packing things away.

"I'm sorry, Krista. I had no right."

"No, you didn't," I said, feeling a pinch in my neck as I reached up to place the box on top of a stack.

"Here, let me—" Dane began.

"No, I've got it."

He was silent then, waiting for me to finish.

I methodically put the chair and other boxes away, picked up the Bible and package of letters, pulled down the door, and locked it. "Will you drop me at Elena's?"

"Sure."

He opened the door for me. I climbed into the front seat, staring straight out the front window as he entered and turned the key. He looked over at me—I could feel the heat of his gaze. "Will you forgive me?"

"Sure," I quipped, repeating his word.

We drove the rest of the way in silence. I hated it, all of it—my anger, his frustration, our mutual discomfort—but I wasn't ready to let it go. I was too riled up inside, my heart too shredded to start feeling again, to start truly forgiving.

Even after all these years the combination of Mother and Dane had sent me reeling.

I need to call my counselor, I thought. But he was away on vacation. This time I was entirely on my own.

1973

Bing Crosby crooned over the radio while I made my mother eggs and toast. She needed to get up and shower. She needed to get to work at the gallery or we'd never be able to buy Oma and Opa Christmas presents. The radio was playing Christmas music all the time now. School was almost out on break. We didn't have much time.

I frowned when I turned the eggs. Mother didn't like her eggs brown at all. "Over easy!" she'd shout. "That means barely done!"

Maybe she'd be too sick this morning to notice. I pulled out the tray and placed a cup of Sanka coffee on it, black like she liked it, the eggs, and a slice of toast with marmalade spread over it. Then, with my tongue perched on the corner of my lips to help me balance, I made my way down the hall and into Mother's darkened bedroom.

"Mother?" I called softly. "It's time to get up." She hated getting up on Saturdays. And she'd been drinking last night. There was a small glass bottle beside her on the bed, lid off, empty. "Mother?"

She moaned and turned over, lifted a hand to her forehead. "What time is it?" she mumbled. The room stank of body odor and liquor.

"Nine. You have to go to work at ten. I made you some breakfast."

She squinched one eye closed and lifted the other eyelid to peer out at me. "Eggs?"

"And toast. With marmalade."

"With marmalade?"

"Yeah."

She opened both eyes then and wearily sat up. She took the tray from me and then gave me a rare smile. "You really are a good kid, Krista."

"Really?"

"Really," she said, biting into the toast.

Chapter Three

December 14

After years of teaching twentieth-century history classes, I knew what Mother's life would most likely have been like after her marriage to Lieutenant Gordon Cooper in 1942. From the looks of their wedding picture, positioned, unframed, between the pages of the Christmas carol book, she had been living frugally with her parents. Nice, slim ivory suit for her vows, probably had traced-on hosiery lines down the back of her long, slender legs. She looked impossibly young, way too young to marry, way too young to be a widow in the making.

She had waited four years for Gordon to come home. In that time she had started her own dance studio, which later flourished, and dabbled with the town's "in crowd." But that success did little to heal her pain over her husband's absence. Gordon took her heart overseas and never returned. Marcellin, my father, did the same.

What had that dual impact done to her? My mind switched back to 1942, back to the innocent couple in the picture.

Eight million households had had sons in the military and bore the star of the service flag in their windows with pride. Lights were dimmed on the highest buildings of coastal cities, unwilling to give away the location of their ships to enemy U-boats. Dress was conservative, the only real differentiation being fabric and frills. Air-raid sirens made a debut across the American landscape. One hundred and ten thousand Japanese-Americans had been herded into "relocation" centers. Undoubtedly my own family faced some persecution with a Germanic name like Mueller and the outcry against Hitler reaching full swing. Maybe they sheltered under mother's new married name of Cooper. She had probably kept things simple then, adding her bit to the war effort, keeping up appearances.

Or maybe she had truly been frugal then. Maybe she had been different, willing to sacrifice some of self…

The Christmas carol book contained a passage from 1942:

Mama and Poppa's lives have always been so perfect. As soon as they were married, they never parted. Mama says that the only time they've ever been apart was for ten days. Gordon and I were married four days before he left. I will always treasure those four perfect days, our tiny rented pueblo outside Santa Fe, the wonders of being a married woman. But now he's been gone for months, and there's no sign of the war letting up. The Japanese bombed Santa Barbara. Clark Gable's even signed up now, and he's forty-one!

Gordon writes from time to time, but I long for him to

return, for him to come home, for us to start our lives together. Poppa says I should start my own dance studio, keep my mind off my husband's absence. But with service stars in windows everywhere I look, how can I keep my mind off him?

As I wrap a present for him, I wonder if he'll even be alive when it arrives. It is constant terror to live with this fear.

I set aside the book and picture and sighed. I knew what was to come for Charlotte Mueller. They never even sent Gordon's body home. And the resulting pang of sorrow for her confused me. I chided myself. Didn't everyone deserve a measure of empathy? Even my mother?

She was laboring on today with little change, still unresponsive. What was I doing here anyway? What was all this digging going to get me? Do for me?

Stir-crazy, suddenly hungry, I pulled the next three letters from the stack—what appeared to be letters from Gordon—and decided it was time to grab some lunch. Taking my coat and purse, I muttered toward Mother, "I'll be back in a couple of hours."

As I left Cimarron's front doors, I took a deep breath, feeling as though I hadn't really breathed all morning. I walked quickly to my car, appreciating the brisk air and the uncharacteristic clouds that covered the valley. It suited my mood. Pensive. Grumbly.

The Prelude roared to life after a hesitation, courtesy of a new hole in my muffler and a starter motor that had been acting up lately. I'd have to stop by Robbie's shop for an estimate soon. Robbie was Elena's son, a friend, but he wasn't Dane.

❧

"You've seen your mama this morning?" Elena said as soon as I came in. I dropped my purse and hung my coat on the rack beside the door, then slid onto a barstool. Elena bustled around the kitchen, barely looking at me.

"Yes. She's about the same as yesterday."

"H'm. With that death rattle in her chest, I am surprised she is still with us." She dished up a bowl of leftover chicken chili and handed it to me without asking if I cared for any. Doña Elena always assumed one was hungry when one entered her home. She was usually right.

"Dane said I had to come right away. But I can't tell if it was because he was really afraid that she might die any day or because he wanted me to see the book."

"He gave you her Christmas notes then?"

I concentrated on taking a cold muffin from the basket she set on the counter instead of looking at her. She was suddenly still, obviously full of expectation. It made me mildly defensive. "He did."

"And?"

"And I'm reading them. Slowly," I added, making myself not shrug and squirm under her gaze. I was, after all, thirty-seven. *Thirty-seven,* I repeated to myself.

"They're for you, my Krista. Her last Christmas gift to you."

I mused over that a moment, then looked up at her. "Are you not eating?"

"I already ate." She was fingering the silver pendant hanging on a chain around her neck, one she had probably made herself. It was angular, like a design from an Apache pot. I prepared myself for an object lesson. Doña Elena reveled in her object lessons. Had they not been usually applicable and had I not found myself constantly referring to her wisdom through the years, I would have tuned her out. I watched as her lips formed the words like bullets—not soft-hearted, tender phrases—that would be discharged.

"Silver is much like us," she said softly. "It needs to be refined by fire before it becomes the beautiful metal we love. Your mother went through many fires, dear one."

"Doesn't everyone? And I'm not seeing much beauty at the end, Doña Elena. She was a bitter old woman before her time. Those fires," I said, waving toward her necklace, "made her a burned-out coal of a woman, not something beautiful."

"It takes coal some pressure and time to make a diamond," she said.

I sat back and looked at her, then out the window. "If there's a diamond deep inside, I never saw a glimpse of it."

She rose then. "You better start mining then, child. Time is short."

I returned to Cimarron that afternoon to spend more time in Charlotte's silent presence, silent except for her breathing, which was loud and unsettling. I mostly stared out the window at the mountains and puttered about the room, setting out old decorations from the Christmas box in Mother's room.

It had been the memory boxes outside each room and other patients' lovingly decorated abodes that had made me think of making the place look festive. Elena had set up a decent memory box on the wall just outside Mother's door—a shadow box with a baby picture of Charlotte, a picture of Oma and Opa with Mother as a girl out on the ranch, a picture of me as a baby in her arms in the mid '60s. There was a diploma from some dance school I'd never heard of, the logo for her dance studio—with the dates "1943–1949" on a banner above it—an ornate Navajo silver pin she used to wear, a bulletin from her church. There was a small crucifix and news clippings of her marriage to Gordon Cooper and a later announcement of her marriage to Marcellin. It was a fair representation of her life.

But as I rummaged back through the Christmas decorations, I realized it was after Oma and Opa had died that Mother refused to decorate for Christmas. When I was a kid, it seemed that she had never decorated. But now I realized it was only after their death that the Christmas decorations remained stored. One year I begged for weeks for a tree, and a few days before Christmas, she brought home a small, bedraggled Charlie Brown Christmas tree. I was elated.

I had pulled out the old handblown glass ornaments and even strung popcorn, like they taught us in elementary school. I cut out paper snowflakes and crafted a three-dimensional star of construction paper for the top. Mother had come in then, weaving drunkenly on her feet. She took one look at that tree and burst into tears.

We never had a tree again.

I pulled out the old glass ornaments now and strung them on a long, thick ribbon and hung them in looping intervals from the top of her window. They looked merry hanging there, festive. I could almost pretend for a moment that we had been a normal family, that these were beloved memories from her past.

I stared at them, slightly turning in the subtly circulating air, until darkness covered the sky behind the window.

Still Mother labored on, breathing in and out, her lungs thick with mucus.

"I'm heading home for a soak in the hot tub. Want to join me?" Dane said from the doorway.

We had spoken little since our run-in the day before. He had been conspicuously absent all day, and I was anxious to set things at ease. I didn't want to spend my whole time here at odds with him. He was, after all, one of my oldest friends. When I paused, he said, "We don't even have to talk. I just thought it might feel good to you. If your day was anything like mine, that is."

"I need to stop by Elena's for my swimsuit. Then I'll be over." I didn't mention dinner. I wasn't up to any candlelight tonight.

"All right," he said. "See you when I see you."

I rose and gathered my things, then stopped at the nurses' station. No one was there, so I jotted down my cell number and the request to call immediately if anything changed.

I drove over to Dane's. The man walked to CCC most days himself, crossing on a well-worn serpentine path through the sagebrush, only driving when the snow was too deep or he had someplace else to go. There was a less-worn path from Elena's to

CCC, but still I elected to drive. Life itself seemed like an effort these days. To bushwhack my way over to Dane's at night, risking limb or rattlesnake, seemed beyond my capacity.

It took me all of three minutes to get there. Welcoming warm light poured from Dane's cozy pueblo. The front porch was fashioned from large, rough-hewn timbers. In the summer, I knew, Dane would usually be found outside, choosing to entertain or be by himself, for that matter, on the patio. There were large, plain windows on all sides to take advantage of his phenomenal view of mountains meeting desert. I could see him in the kitchen, tinkering.

I ducked away before he could see me spying and knocked on the door.

He answered it, wearing a beat-up long-sleeved T-shirt and a beach towel around his hips. "I made some nachos. Hope you don't mind casual food."

"Never have," I said, moving beside him. I felt a wave of electricity at his nearness, a shock of awareness. *I shouldn't be here,* I realized. I should have elected for some time alone in Elena's sauna. But to be under the stars, soaking my tension away… Dane and I were friends. I had to keep it straight in my head, or this whole trip would be misery. He certainly wasn't looking for anything more. Not if he was smart.

I swallowed an "I'm not that hungry" when I smelled the melted cheese and chips. They smelled and looked divine. He moved past me and grabbed a cookie sheet piled with layers of chips and cheddar and chilies. "Got your suit on?"

"Yes."

"Grab a drink and let's go. I don't know about you, but I can't wait to get into that steaming water and do nothing but stare up at the stars."

"Me neither," I said. It was good, this goal. If he only wanted silence and hot water and stars, he wouldn't spend his time analyzing me. I opened his refrigerator and searched for a Coke. By the time I emerged, he was gone, the open door the only trace of his path. *Guess he's got nothing but water and food on his mind either.*

I looked around his comfortable living room and kitchen. It was all traditional Southwest, done in contemporary fashion. Spare, leather furniture, the color of milk chocolate. Curved iron tables with large glass tops. Copies of *Architectural Digest* fanned out with precision. Large red clay tiles on the floor. A huge kiva fireplace in the corner, raised up for maximum viewing. Several intriguing sculptures—

"Krista!" he shouted.

"Yeah?" I asked, as if just heading out instead of snooping.

"Grab me a soda, will you?"

"Sure." I headed back to the kitchen and chose a Mountain Dew for Dane.

I left my shoes in the house and scurried over the ice-cold brick tiles of the patio to the hot tub. Dane was already settled in, a few fat candles lit around the perimeter. I was glad there were no other lights on. I felt as though I weighed three hundred pounds.

My counselor told me I had been borderline anorexic as a kid.

Probably still struggled with the tendencies. She said it was directly attributable to my feelings of inadequacy and not living up to my mother's expectations…

I groaned.

"What?" Dane said, head back against the headrest, spread out across one end of the Jacuzzi. He didn't look in my direction, seeming to sense my need for space, privacy.

"Nothing. Oh, but this water. Man, that feels good." I dipped my feet into the water, wincing a little at the heat, but, once seated, glad for its soothing work. My hair spread out in waves around my shoulders, and I sank down until the water reached my neck.

"Nachos?" he offered.

I moved over to the tray between us and pulled off a chip mounded with rapidly cooling cheese. The salty taste was marvelous, especially when I doused the heat of the chilies with some cola. "What are you doing for Christmas?" I asked.

"Guess I'll be with the gang at Cimarron. Mom and Dad are going on a cruise. My sister will be with the in-laws in New England."

"Have you spent many Christmases alone?"

"No," he said, eyeing me briefly. "The last two times my family abandoned me over the holidays I was with someone."

"Ah." With someone. I had no right to ask.

"What about you?"

"Mostly with friends, other faculty. People who feel sorry for the single girl with no family in town."

Dane nodded. Then, "No boyfriends?"

"No," I confirmed. Never any man. There really had never been any man except Dane. Friends. Interested parties. Even interesting interested parties. But no one quite up to par with Dane McConnell. Not that I would tell him that.

My counselor said I was afraid of men.

I said I was just picky.

We ate the rest of the chips in companionable silence and sat back to watch the stars emerge from their velvet nap. We were far enough outside of town not to have to compete with its lights, to be able to see such a vast astronomic display that we could make out the outline of Taos Mountain silhouetted against the stars, even without benefit of a moon. High above, a hawk screeched as it circled above us, and in the distance we heard a coyote yipping.

"It's good to have you home, Kristabelle."

"It's…good to be here." And it was. It really was.

The years that followed Oma and Opa's death yawned wide with our shared pain and loss. One day when I was twelve, heating Hungry Man dinners in the oven for our Christmas lunch, I realized that Mother was up out of bed for the first time in a week. Following a trail of open doors, I discovered her in the backyard, crazily throwing out box after box of stored goods from our storage shed.

"Mother?" I asked. "What are you doing?" I was a little frightened by the frantic activity, the wild light in her eyes.

"I'm cleaning it out!" She disappeared again to grab another box. She was still in her nightgown at one in the afternoon. It was only fifty degrees out.

"For what? Maybe you should get some clothes—"

"For you! For you, my darling." She was suddenly right there, pulling me close, hugging me so tightly I couldn't breathe. It had been months since she had embraced me. I froze.

I couldn't figure out what she meant. Did she think I would sleep out here?

She laughed then, studying my face. Laughed madly. "Don't you see? This is exactly what I need! What we need!"

"Wh-what?"

"I'm going to teach you to dance. You have my body, my movements. You'll be perfect, darling! I'm going to open my dance studio again, and you will be my first student."

"What about the gallery?"

"I gave them notice. Merry Christmas!" She threw her arms around me in another hug.

"Gave them notice? Quit?"

"Yes. This will be much better for us, you'll see. People are beginning to notice how much the Southwest has to offer; they'll want to know more of New Mexico's roots. What better way than the old dances?"

I stood there, torn between the warming glory of my mother's sudden, effusive love and the sheer panic of wondering how we'd afford our next frozen dinner. Things seemed tight enough, though Mother always had enough cash to throw a party or go drinking.

"Darling," she said, emerging from the shed again and gleefully tossing another carton, "come and help me! This is for us!"

There was such promise in my mother's eyes, such unaccustomed happiness, that I wanted to believe her. I immediately abandoned the Hungry Man dinners to their doom and set to work beside her.

CHAPTER FOUR

December 15

As America shifted from post–World War II cleanup to the Cold War against the communists—we were taught as kids that the owner built a bomb shelter under the Taos Inn—and from casseroles to meat five nights a week, my mother was still mourning her husband. Four million veterans took advantage of the GI bill in 1947 and its tracks toward housing, education, and business. Gordon was not one of them. I found this letter under Martin and Blane's famous tune of 1944, "Have Yourself a Merry Little Christmas":

December 1947

I long to return to the Christmases of my youth, when I had hopes and dreams and love in my heart. Now only darkness fills my soul. Oh, foul world that would take my prince and reduce him to so little that could identify him! By night I am haunted by veterans' stories of capture and torture by the Japanese. By day my mind traverses to the horrible motion pictures shown at the Nuremberg trials of corpses and living skeletons freed from concentration camps. Did he look like that in the end? Surely my Gordon went through hell before he died. Did he perish thinking of me? Of God? Where in all of creation was God when such nightmares came to life?

I try to focus on my dream of a dance studio, of developing little girls into dancers. But how can I dance when my shoulders droop from the burden of Gordon's suffering? Poppa says he'll help me. He intends to sell all but a few of the sheep and has accepted a job downtown at the hardware store. Mama says it's important that I find myself, my own life again. Because they see what I know—that I am lost, lost, lost.

Her anguish made me swallow hard, the first full measure of empathy I'd had for Mother in many years. Except, of course, when it came to her Alzheimer's. Her descent into the mind-thief had been a sorry thing to witness; no one, not even Mother, deserved the indignities of the disease. Wrist watches in sugar bowls, keys in the bath salts, missed appointments, forgotten names, disorientation to the point that she could not remember her way home from a block away. Embarrassment at the store when she could not recall where the milk was shelved; humiliation in the women's shoe department when she asked for a size five shoe for her size seven foot.

Mother had seldom been kind before, but she had always been sharp as a new knife when it came to brains. For her to lose her mental faculties was particularly pitiful. When she could no longer remember the steps to her favorites dances, it was downright tragic. I looked over at her, laboring for breath in her hospital bed, her eyes empty and unblinking. She had loved, truly loved Gordon. Maybe even more than my father. How had that loss changed her?

Hesitating a moment, I leaned forward and took her hand. Her fingers were cold and frail, the skin like wrinkly vellum over blue arteries. There was no response. "I'm sorry, Mother," I said softly. "I'm sorry you lost Gordon. It must've hurt you very much."

There was no answer. Not that I expected one really. I squeezed her hand and then released it just as Mother's doctor, the slim, pretty brunette I'd seen through the window, entered the room. "Ah," she said, appraising me, "you must be Charlotte's daughter." Her eyes shifted to the monitor and IV stand that banked the head of my mother's bed, then to her chart.

"I am. Krista Mueller. Are you her doctor?"

"Indeed. Suzanne Cunningham," she said, as if an afterthought, reaching across my mother to briefly shake my hand. She was immediately intent on listening to Charlotte's lungs and looking back at the monitors. As she made some notes on the chart, she spoke to me. "You're a good friend of Dane's, right?"

I noticed her use of his first name.

"Neighbor as a kid. High school sweethearts once. But those days are over."

"Ah. I see. First loves—they're always tough to forget." She was checking me out. I was sure of it. Too careful in her word choice, telltale split-second pauses that betrayed her interest. I had seen her look out the window after us. The woman was fighting jealousy.

"It all was a long time ago. We're just friends," I said. "If you're into him, he's all yours."

"Oh, I, uh…I was simply curious. I have no interest in Dr. McConnell. That would be…highly unprofessional."

"M'm," I said in agreement. *Dr. McConnell* was it now? A moment ago it was *Dane.* The doctor's eyes met mine for a moment. She knew I knew she was bluffing. Just one of the minions that would fall for Dane while he was alive.

"How's Mother?" I said, letting her off the hook.

Dr. Cunningham's expression showed the mental shift from Dane to Mother, as if surprised to be yanked back into reality. *Hello, my mother's on her deathbed here. Keep your mind on her, would you, Doc?* "Yes, m'm. It's not good. Dane's told you she has little time left, hasn't he?"

Dane again. Why did it rankle me? "Yes, he has."

Her tone gentled. "It could be anytime now. We are doing our best to alleviate some of her congestion, but it's a never-ending battle, Krista. Kind of like bailing water out of a sinking boat. Her heart is failing and can't accept the blood sent from her lungs fast enough to get rid of it. We can fight back, but for only so long."

I nodded in understanding. "Whatever you can do to make her more comfortable…"

"We are pursuing every available resource."

"How do you know what's best when the patients can't tell you how they feel?"

"We're pretty adept at treating symptoms. We've learned to read the body language of pain, discomfort. Have to around here."

I nodded again. "Thank you, Doctor."

"Anytime." She reached into the white pocket of her lab coat and pulled out a business card. "I'm sure you know that an RN is always on duty to monitor Charlotte's vitals at the station in the hall. And when I'm not on the Cimarron campus, I'm just ten minutes away at the hospital. Dane said you'd rather have your mother here instead of the hospital. Is that correct?"

Dane. "Correct. As long as she's as comfortable as possible, I think it's better for her to live her last days here."

It was her turn to nod. There was a measure of empathy in her eyes that I liked. Dane would like that, I thought. They probably were made for each other. What was holding him back? I cleared my throat. "You'll tell me if you could do more for her at the hospital?"

"With a do-not-resuscitate order, there's little I could do there that I can't do here. I agree that she's better off here. More homey at least. And I'm here every morning." She paused a moment, then reached out to shake my hand. "I must look in on the others," she said in salutation.

"It was nice to meet you, Dr. Cunningham. Thanks for taking care of my mother."

"Of course."

My eyes shifted back to my mother as the doctor leaned down to whisper good-bye to her, squeezed her hand, then left the room. A doctor who used a word like *homey* was the right kind to have. The kind I'd want if I couldn't speak, entombed in a decaying body while my mind remained restlessly awake. I took Charlotte's hand and bowed my head for the thousandth time in prayer. *This must be the end, huh, Lord? She's been through enough. Take her home, Father. Bring her to wholeness again. Release her. Please, Jesus. Release her. Amen.*

But the heart monitor still betrayed a steady beat.

Sifting through Charlotte's words made me feel like a bit of a voyeur. After staring at the heart monitor for about five minutes, I finally rose, intent on stretching my legs and getting my mind off her for a bit. I waved at Annie, the nurse, and an aide I didn't recognize conferring in the station near my mother's room—there was a station and a nurse on every wing. I stooped to pat Spartacus, the guard dog on the Eisenhower wing, and moved toward the arboretum. It was sleeting outside in a sudden change of weather, and I chose to stay indoors today.

Dane had designed Cimarron to be conducive to an Alzheimer's patient's need to roam. Constantly they were on their feet, setting off for somewhere. The trick was to at once accommodate that urge *and* keep them safe. Cimarron was perfect for it. The hallways led to winding paths among three indoor gardens. Along the walkways were boxes full of plastic flowers the residents could "pick" and take to the nurses or their neighbors or to their own room. Higher up, just out of reach, were real plants and flowers. And above it all were twenty-year-old trees, transplanted indoors to lend an authentic garden feel. Aides rotated through every five or ten minutes to make sure patients weren't becoming agitated in their wanderings. They helped those that were lost find their way back to their rooms.

Mr. Wallace was already there. Mother's next-door neighbor had been at Cimarron as long as she had, one of the facility's first residents. Five years ago he had been able to communicate fairly well. "Lost my rudder," he had explained back then. Getting lost about Taos had become an everyday occurrence. When he ended up in a riverbed at night, wet from head to toe, his daughter had called Dane.

I searched my brain for his first name, conscious that the staff always referred to patients that way. "How are you feeling, Peter?" I asked as I neared.

"With my fingers."

I smiled at the well-worn quip and took his arm when he offered it. "Off on a walk, are we? Where are we heading?"

"Somewhere west of east."

I grinned again. "That's good, good. I needed to stretch my legs." We walked in companionable silence for a bit, and I wondered if he was trying to figure out who in the world he was escorting. "My mother, Charlotte, isn't doing well," I said. "I think your neighbor might be nearing the end of her days."

He paused and plucked a garish red plastic geranium from a pot and handed it to me. "I'll assume that's for Mother," I said. "I'm much too young for you, Peter."

He smiled, as purely pleased as a young buck caught in a fanciful moment of flirtation. By the dim look in his eyes, I could tell he was still completely confused but happy. Where was he in time? Courting his wife in the '40s? I could be Rosie the Riveter for a bit if it would help. When dealing with Alz, one learns to seize the happy moments.

We strolled onward. At the end of the hall was a glass wall with long windows that showed the berm outside and several bird feeders. There was another dignified old gent sitting nearby before an empty chessboard. He held his chin in hand as if contemplating the next move. But there were no pieces, no competitor.

Another patient was around the next curve, lying down on the green "grass" that was really cheap plastic turf. She was dressed in a pretty cotton sundress and stared upward through the tree branches to the sleet hitting the glass panes as if spring sunlight streamed down on her face.

I pulled Mr. Wallace to a halt. "Ma'am?" I asked the woman. "Are you all right?" She waved me away as if I were a pesky bee invading her idyllic picnic reverie.

Mr. Wallace and I continued on our walk. In a minute we had reached the end of the path where it entered the hall. Several silk plants divided the exit from the entry, making it more of an effort for patients to reenter the path into the arboretum. Otherwise, Dane had explained, patients might grow agitated, feeling lost, circling the garden over and over, unable to "get home." In this manner those who could remember the way could enter the arboretum again. Others would do a loop back through their wing—and past their caregivers—before heading back. "Going back to your room?" I asked my escort.

He took off his sharp fedora and gave me a gallant bow of dismissal. Then he turned and walked around the plant, entering the gardens again. So, he had remembered. Slices of memory in Alz patients often emerged in sudden displays that were as surprising and delightful as a glimpse of a baby bird in a nest. Mother had given such glimpses a long time ago. His departure made me feel lonely.

When I looked up, I spied Dane, leaning against the far wall, grinning at me as if I had just given him a longed-for present. He neared me and looked after Peter. "That was nice, what you did."

"Taking a spin with Mr. Wallace?" I shrugged a little. "Felt good."

"You are good with the patients, Krista." He looked at me then deeply, as if searching for something hidden behind my eyes.

"All except my own mother."

He headed back with me then to Charlotte's room. "Sometimes it's hardest with the people closest to us. We can give others a little more space, a little more leeway, but when it comes to our own..."

"They get the brunt of it." Dane glanced at me, but I refused to look at him. "I did the best I could with her, Dane."

"I know it."

"She's never been easy."

"I know."

We turned the corner of Eisenhower, and Dane paused and, like Peter before him, bowed and doffed an imaginary fedora too.

I shook my head and smiled.

Dane leaned close to my ear. "It was a nice thing you did," he repeated. And then he swiveled on his heel and disappeared.

I didn't see Dane the rest of that day and chastised myself for wondering where he went. I had no right to keep tabs on the man, no reason to wonder. I had been friendly enough since my arrival, but I was intent on avoiding our endless pattern of flirtation and infatuation before ultimately parting again. I didn't want to be hurt this time, or hurt him. Last night had been good, but I didn't intend to see him much. Hadn't I just told Suzanne that I held no claim on his heart? I'd practically invited the woman to go for him.

I sat in Mother's room for an hour, staring out at the cloud-shrouded mountains and the endless dripping of the skies. I had not the mental energy or the emotional capacity to further enter her history today. After a moment I rose and walked to the small CD player I had bought for her room and chose *Siesta Suite* from among the discs in my travel case. The soothing sounds of Spanish guitar and flute filled the air. Steps to a traditional *valse* made my feet itch to move.

I leaned forward in my chair and patted my mother's arm in

time with the beat. "Remember, Mother? Remember when you danced to these songs? You were beautiful when you danced. Alive." I could give her these gifts of compliments. I could do this, at least, for the woman.

The music reminded me of the signs I'd seen about town shouting news of the First Annual Navidad Town Square Dance. Entry to the region always left me thinking of dance. It was ingrained in me; for as long as I could remember, I had danced. But not for years. Not since I had left Mother and New Mexico and Dane for Colorado.

I squeezed Mother's arm and gave her a dutiful kiss on the temple. "Good-bye, Mother. I'll be back tomorrow." It was all I could bear for the day—I was wound up tight inside. I left the music playing, feeling as melancholy as the sorry tune. It was the gray day, I told myself. Rain always made me feel sleepy and a bit depressed. A mother on her deathbed didn't help either...

I waved at Annie and ignored Spartacus's dutiful, lumbering gait toward me, suddenly wanting nothing but the spare, comforting simplicity of my room at Elena's in this crowded, crazy world. I couldn't help but glance down the hallway of the administrative and doctors' offices as I passed through "Main Street." No sign of Dane. Maybe Suzanne had taken my advice and asked him out.

Outside, without either umbrella or hood, I dashed for my car, trying to avoid the deepest puddles of half-frozen muddy water. Fortunately I had been able to park close. I yanked open the creaking door and slammed it behind me, my huffing breath visible in small clouds.

It was then that I saw the large package in the passenger seat. The box was wrapped in silver foil paper with a white ribbon; an elegant, small envelope was tucked underneath. I wiped my hand on my jeans, not wanting to get it wet, and then reached for it. *Dane.* It had to be.

Sure enough, his small, tight script filled the card.

An early Christmas present. I only have one request of Santa this year. That you will meet me at the town square for one dance. Just one, Kristabelle.

Swallowing hard, I tore open the wrap. Inside was the most gorgeous blouse, long skirt, and matching shawl that I had seen in years. It reminded me of a picture of Mother wearing something similar when she was young and in demand as a dance instructor. The white linen blouse could be worn on or off the shoulder and boasted handmade lace along its edge. The bodice was slim, made to tuck into the wide waistband of the skirt, which was cut on the bias to billow out properly and swirl with the dance steps. Its fabric was more sedate than the typical Spanish patterns and colors but all the more unique because of it. The shawl was of uneven, handmade yarns in shades of greens and browns with a slight sheen. I ran my hand over it, relishing its texture.

He had asked me for just one dance. What could one dance hurt? Did I have the will power to decline his invitation?

But oh, to dance with him again! It had been years, but the guitar strings and flutes and maracas and violins were already playing through my head. And to see him in costume again—he could sweep any girl off her feet wrapped inside a billowing full shirt and slim pants.

I had first met Dane when he showed up to take lessons with my mother. I had had a hunch that he was a natural. By the second lesson, I knew I was right. To watch him move across the floor was like watching a Spanish bullfighter drawing near to claim his prize. He had utterly no inhibitions, content to do whatever Mother asked—moving his hips, striding and strutting, clapping... For heaven's sake, my heart was thumping at the memory! But to be in his arms, making the romantic, small movements that made Spanish folk dancing all it was, raising my eyes to meet his gaze...

No. No! I let out a cry of disgust, ran my hands through my damp hair, and shook my head in frustration with myself. I tossed the package to the passenger seat. There was no way I was going to the town dance with Dane McConnell. No way I would meet him there. It was best for both of us if I steered clear of it altogether. It was the best, the right way. Otherwise, we'd be back where we always started, always ended. In ecstasy, in agony.

I turned the key in the ignition. It was right, this decision. *Right, Lord? Help me out a little here.*

But as I drove out of Cimarron, I felt nothing but loss.

For Mother. For Dane. For me.

We had practiced and practiced for the 1978 Christmas recital. Mother had managed to scrape together twelve students, eight girls and four boys. By living on cheap soup and beans, she never returned to her work at the gallery.

Her old friends, people who had abandoned her in the early 1960s when she quit teaching dance, came back around, and for a while Mother managed to stay out of bed during the day. She kept late hours with the artsy crowd, often spending an entire week's budget on one night of wine and song, but to see my mother this happy was worth it to me.

I worked especially hard on the chote, *knowing that Mother planned to pair me with Miguel Esquibel, the most handsome boy in my eighth grade class and a natural dancer. He was attending my mother's classes under duress. I knew if I flubbed the steps and made him look more conspicuous than he already was at recital, he would never look my way again.*

So I practiced in my room at night, in the kitchen before school, for hours afterward. My mother gave me nods of approval when she discovered how hard I worked, and I reveled in it. This was good, right. Mother and I were finally doing okay together.

All was going well through the recital until I met up with Miguel for the chote and he took my hands in his. My heart was hammering so fast I could barely see. Dimly I heard the music start and automatically began to follow Miguel's lead in the sideways shuffling steps, right-left-right. But when we got to the next section and assumed the ballroom position, I fell apart. Miguel did his best to keep me on track, but to no avail. I practically tripped him.

Mother stood up in the center front row before about fifty people. I heard women gasp. I noticed other kids slowing to a stop and gazing my direction. Mother was staring only at me. Finally Miguel stopped too and looked at Mother, then the ground. Horrified, I dared to meet her gaze.

"Fool!" she hissed. "You have ruined it all! Ruined it! Get off that stage! Get off the stage right now!"

Chapter Five

December 16

In the year Adlai Stevenson said, "Some of us worship in churches, some in synagogues, some on golf courses," my mother became immersed in Native American spirituality. I found it intriguing that during a time when Charlotte rejected the faith of her parents, she was still writing in the book of Christmas carols and, in particular, beneath "God Rest Ye Merry Gentlemen" with its words of Christ's and Satan's power.

Maybe she wasn't as sure as she sounded. After all, I knew she later proclaimed to be a Christian, even if she didn't seem to practice her beliefs. By the time I was born, there was little evidence of her quest, other than a few telltale books gathering dust on a shelf. In the last twenty years, the only book on religion I'd seen my mother open was the Bible. Maybe she had eventually settled on the solace that it alone could bring to a wandering soul. Her entry:

December 1952

I finally feel as if I've found where I belong. My dance studio is thriving, and I've earned enough to live on my own. Emancipation from my parents' home has given me the gift of freedom on other fronts: I spend my evenings with friends, taking in some cool jazz at the Tony Room; I've gone on dates with the most fascinating men about town (usually in Santa Fe. Taos is full of cowboys, not my type at all!); I've taken to entertaining guests for dinner with conversation that stimulates the mind. Poppa would frown on the cloud of cigarette smoke that fills my rooms, but I revel in it. My Sunday mornings are spent relaxing and recuperating from our late Saturday night "extravaganzas," as Philippe refers to them, not that I am not pursuing spiritual interests. Of late, I am reading books by leading people of all devout faiths—Buddhist, Muslim, Jewish, Christian. But what captures my interest the most is the people of my land—the Pueblos who actually go below ground to their kivas to encounter Mother Earth. The people who wait for her to water our land and produce the bounty that feeds them.

My life is so utterly different now. At thirty I finally have found who I am meant to be. And it's not who my parents tried to make me. It is who I am. Sensual. Intriguing. Strong. Talented. Alive.

This Christmas will not be spent in my parents' dull house. Philippe is taking me away. I am not in love with him, nor he with me. We merely amuse each other, but I am not interested in being tied down. We are content, constant companions for now.

I let out a sound of exasperation. Part of me was proud of my mother for emerging from her daze of dark depression following Gordon's death, much as she did later when we unpacked the storage unit to make way for the return of her dance studio. I was proud of her for finding her own place in the world in a time when it was all about finding a man. Not that she hadn't… *Philippe*. Foreign and smart sounding. Who had he been? Had they been intimate? Up to now I had never even heard his name.

But beyond her casual relationships with men, a part of me was even more sickened by her path of wandering, her entry into what I always called the Valley of Self. Charlotte Mueller never fully emerged from that Valley. It was forevermore all about her, all the time. Even when I came along.

My eyes traced the paragraph about Philippe. Where had he taken her? Perhaps a brochure or something in the storage unit would tip me off. I could just see them all, on cushions around her living room, smoking cigarette after cigarette, drinking too much, fancying their conversation as brighter and more amusing than if they had been sober. I could see my mother dressed in a narrow skirt and the old mink stole I had discovered, on the arm of a man in a jazz club. I could see her cultivating friendships with the in-crowd about town, collecting them just as surely as Mabel Dodge

Luhan had, as much as to try to fill an inexplicable emptiness within them as out of genuine interest in the arts.

It was Mabel who had invited Georgia O'Keeffe to Taos in 1929, Mabel who had given an old Kiowa ranch to D. H. and Frieda Lawrence. Lawrence, in turn, gave her his original manuscript for *Sons and Lovers*. In similar fashion I knew Mother had cultivated the artisans around her, joining the Taos Art Association, lobbying for the Encore Theatre that was built three years later. In 1952 one of Taos's great artists, Oscar Berninghaus, died. And yet there was no mention of him in her Christmas note. Odd. She had taken great pride in becoming a confidante of Millicent Rogers, once the subject of photographs in *Vogue* and *Harper's Bazaar,* and grieved her death in 1953. Or so she had told me in later years.

The thought of Millicent sent me to her jewelry box on the dresser in the corner of her room. I opened it, bracing myself to find it empty, but there, underneath several cheap costume jewelry necklaces, was the silver-and-turquoise pin Millicent had bequeathed her. It was a magnificent piece, probably very old Navajo workmanship, circa 1900. I pinned it on my sweater, thinking I'd show it to Elena and see if she agreed. Mother wouldn't miss it.

I glanced at it again and thought of Elena's words about silver and refining. What had refined Mother during those years? What had been the fire that made her stronger, refined her silver?

By 1952 Taos had been officially discovered, and the tourist boom began. Armed with station wagons and Kodak cameras, they came to pose in front of Kit Carson's house, try the local food, and, if they were really daring, review the Lawrence paintings displayed in La Fonda de Taos—the same paintings banned from Lawrence's native England because they were deemed obscene.

I paced, staring out the window, trying to get a handle on who Mother had been then, what she had been like in such a rapidly changing world. She'd seemed happy, energized. What had happened to bring about the sad-eyed woman I knew as Mother?

I glanced at her laboring form and wished I'd known her then. That woman seemed like someone I might have enjoyed getting to know over coffee, even befriending. She was wild and searching, but at least she had been *living*. Not in the slow-death mode that had come to dominate her days in the last thirty years.

I sat with her for a long time, wondering what might have been.

Finally, my mind still adrift in the world of O'Keeffe and Lawrence, I grabbed my coat and bent to kiss my mother. "I'll be back," I mumbled, heading for the door.

On the road I turned south toward the center of town. As I drove, I knew it was to the San Francisco de Asis church I headed. I rolled down my window and blasted the heater so I could inhale the scents of the piñon pine and winter-dried grasses beneath the snow-capped mountains. The morning had blossomed with a clear winter sun, the Sangre de Cristo range covered in white. Being in Taos frequently reminded me of living amid brilliant cinematography, as if I'd entered one of those beautiful movies like *Far and Away* or *Empire of the Sun* or *Out of Africa*. While my radio remained silent, I could almost hear on the wind the sounds of a solo Native American flute playing haunting, lonely music. R. Carlos Nakai was my favorite, playing the ancient melodies of the Zuni, the Lakota, the Kiowa, the Cheyenne.

This land called one to simplicity. I believed in honoring the native peoples' culture, their respect for this beautiful country, but I didn't get caught up in their beliefs. A part of me empathized with my mother for her wandering heart. Over the course of my own life I had learned to incorporate the native traditions into my own Christian faith where I could.

Lawrence once said that "Taos is a state of mind." I thought it aptly put. This was a land of shifting winds as well as warm stoves. There were centuries of stories in these hills, of peoples conquered, of peoples conquering. The plaza formation had been heavily utilized in this region—many had built their homes close together to present a walled perimeter as a defense against raiders. There was an open area in the middle where one could work or walk and visit out of the wind. What had been lost in our move to single-family dwellings, to fences not shared against a common enemy but erected between us to keep everyone else out?

Had I built my own fences, trained in the art by my mother? Here I was, thirty-seven years old, keeping a high school sweetheart at arm's length and Colorado admirers even further away. I had some good female friends, but I had my walls with them too. What was I doing? Where was I going? At least my mother had found some peace when she hit thirty. My life seemed to keep disintegrating like the old "puddle" adobe, which was prone to collapse under heavy rains. What was the straw that was missing from my adobe? That binding factor that would keep me from totally dissolving?

I laughed at myself. I tended to wax philosophical when I was home. I shook my head and rolled up my window, following the main road until it turned into Paseo del Pueblo Sur, which led to the church O'Keeffe and Paul Strand had made famous in their portraits. San Francisco de Asis had broad hips—the buttresses in back—and welcoming belfries and white crosses in front.

I parked in a nearly empty lot and walked into the courtyard where old pines, contemplative benches, and a statue of Francis of Assisi waited to greet visitors. The architecture of the grand old church was pure Taos—all soft, rounded lines—the adobe painted the color of limestone with a touch of ruddy iron thrown in. Inside, a young Hispanic priest was on his knees praying before the altar. Above him soared a thirty-foot wall *retablo*. The altarpiece glorified the life of Jesus and several saints in various paintings. Each portrait depicted a separate biblical scene. I sat down on a hard wooden bench and took a breath of the musty air that held the faint tinge of incense. Above me were the old, soot-blackened rafters that ended in the subtly decorative style of the region.

I closed my eyes, leaning forward to place my elbows on my knees, my face in my hands. *What, Lord? What do you want from me? I can feel you working on me, trying to tell me something, but what? I know I've been too busy lately, working too hard to spend time listening for you. Please forgive me, Father. Lord, I'm not sure what to do with Mother. I'm at once glad her life is at an end and yet not ready to let her go. There's so much unfinished business between us...*

The scratching sound of paper on wood and the feel of swooshing stiff cotton and air flowing past my face broke into my prayer. The priest was gone from the front and, as I looked backward, on his way out of the church. Did he want to lock up? He gave me no indication that that was what he desired, just disappeared. That was when I saw the half-sheet of paper beside me. It was a flier for *Las Posadas* that would begin tonight, a reenactment of Joseph and Mary's search for shelter during their journey to Bethlehem. It was at Martinez Hacienda, where it had often taken place before.

Even though we weren't Catholic, my grandparents had taken me to quietly join in, following two children dressed as Mary and Joseph, often with Mary on a donkey. We pretended to go from house to house, singing carols. One of the songs they were singing tonight was on the sheet: *"En nombre del cielo, os pido posada, pues no puede andar ya mi esposa amada."* I knew it meant that Mary and Joseph, "in the name of heaven," were asking for shelter. In turn, those in the houses were to reply: *"Aquí no es meson. Sigan adelante pues no puedo abrir no sea algun tunante,"* which meant, in short, "Move along; I can't let you in because you might be a thief or lazy." At that point the people were to shut the doors in their faces.

Taking part in the annual procession had bred in me a deep appreciation for hospitality, of extending help to the less fortunate. I remember crying for them as a six-year-old and Oma wrapping me in her arms and saying, "Don't cry, sweetheart. You know the story. Mary and Joseph find a place for Jesus. Just like we must in our own hearts. We must not shut him out in the cold."

I didn't understand all that it meant at the time. I thought I might now.

I stared upward, longing for Oma and Opa more than I had in a decade. It had been a few years later, when I was ten, that Oma died and, within a month, Opa too. Elena always said that Opa loved Oma so much he could not live without her. I think that when they died, something in my mother died too. She retreated deeper into the Valley of Self that year.

I shivered and hugged myself, suddenly chilled. What, what had been lost? What had shifted within her then? Was it simply being alone in the world, or had her parents kept her more grounded than she liked to think? And why was I so driven to figure it out now as she labored to breathe through her last days?

I left the church and was walking along Ranchitos Road to stretch my legs when Dane pulled up beside me. I couldn't hold back my smile. I was feeling desperately lonely, and my mind shifted from one radical thought to another. His welcoming face made me feel a little warmer, a little more focused. I leaned into the open passenger-side window. It had been Dane who had introduced me to the wonders of lowered car windows and cranked heaters. "Want a ride?" he asked.

I nodded over my shoulder, back toward the parking lot. "My car's back there. You in the habit of cruising for women?"

"Not usually. We just happen to cross paths. I've chalked it up to the Maker's mysterious ways. How 'bout an early dinner?"

I sighed and stared at him. I was hungry. And tempted.

"It's dinner," he said, narrowing his gaze, "not a ruse to get you to the guillotine."

"Oh, in that case, all right. You know how I hate meals that turn into a reason to cut my head off."

"Not today. I promise."

A little levity would be welcome on this day. I was tired of thinking, tired of soul-searching.

"So," Dane said, eyeing me across an intimate table for two at Josef's, the hot, artsy restaurant in town, "what led you to the church?"

"I was thinking. Of Mother and her spiritual quest." My eyes wandered from him to the murals covering the walls, to candles hanging in funky wire holders all about us.

"Is she leaving us for heaven?"

"As much as I can tell. She read her Bible on occasion, and I know she came back to Jesus at one point, but in those last years, when I might've been able to ask her what she believed, I just…didn't." I fiddled with the napkin in my lap, then dared to look at him. I didn't want to talk about my mother anymore. I wanted to talk about anything other than my mother. "What's been keeping you busy?"

"You mean when I'm not stashing presents in people's cars?"

"Yeah." I smiled. "Other than that." We hadn't talked about his gift to me. I hadn't decided on whether or not I'd meet him for that dance. I knew it wasn't smart, that my brain should say no for the sake of my heart, but I couldn't find it within me. For now I'd just try to steer clear of the conversation. Dane knew me well enough not to push. In the dim light his eyes were like the color of sage… Fidgeting, I looked down at my water glass.

"I've been leading a workshop for people just diagnosed with Alz, helping them figure out a game plan, preparing their caregivers for what is to come. And planning our annual think-tank meeting for February."

"It's heavy work, what you do. Mentally, emotionally."

He leaned back in his chair after taking a drink of water. "Somehow it doesn't feel like it to me. Guess that's the gift of doing what you're meant to be doing."

"Like I get excited about taking students to another year, another place, to really *experience* history, you get a charge out of unraveling the secrets of Alz."

"Exactly," he said, nodding this time. He leaned forward, and I fought the urge to lean back, to keep the distance between us. "Our conference will bring in the best scientific and therapeutic minds in the world. Right here, to Taos." He shook his head as though he still couldn't believe it. "Imagine what we can do together!"

I smiled. "You really are a gift, Dane. To so many. I'm glad beyond measure that Mother's at Cimarron. That you were a part of my life before there was a five-year waiting list to get into Cimarron."

He smiled, and I could see the wonder in his eyes. I was softening up, letting him in a little. I had to be more careful. "Are you planning to open new campuses soon?" There was a safe topic. *Good girl.*

"Yes. One in Thousand Oaks, California, come May and in Tallahassee, Florida, in June."

"Will they be just like Cimarron?"

"Similar. I've found excellent locations for each and topnotch directors. We'll try a couple of different therapy techniques in each location, study the effects of the therapies to judge which are most effective."

I could just see him in ten years with a hundred such campuses across the nation. There was no stopping Dane McConnell. He'd never encountered walls in his life, never built them. He was just one big, winding, open path. Was this what a secure childhood, loving parents wrought?

"I met Mother's doctor," I said casually, stirring my hot tea. "She's lovely."

He studied me a moment, then fiddled with his fork. The waiter arrived with our salads, and I knew Dane was glad to have something to do with his utensil. "Suzanne's a great doctor. Efficient. Caring with the patients," he said.

"I could see that." They belonged together. Why couldn't I find it within me to encourage him toward her? Instead, the thought of it made me a little queasy. I stabbed at a tomato like my life depended on it. "Why didn't you ask her to the dance?"

"I didn't want to go with her." He shook his head, took a bite of salad, and studied me again as he chewed. When he finally swallowed, the silence yawning between us like the gorge just east of town, he threw me an amused, knowing look. "You always did try to turn my head toward other women when I was looking your way."

"Dane, I—"

"You always said things like, 'Doesn't Lana Payne look pretty tonight?' or 'Have you noticed that Barb's been working out?' when I started getting too close."

"This is different. You two are colleagues. I was just thinking how perfect it would be—"

"How perfect it would be if you were to join me for that dance?"

"No, I was talking about Suzanne."

"And I was talking about you. You said it; I didn't. Suzanne and I are colleagues. It's hardly professional to date my staff."

"What's a guy supposed to do? You're there. She's there. Common interests and all that." What was I doing? The further this conversation went, the less I felt like eating. Dutifully I took a bite of what my friend Elise called "weeds." It was one of those gourmet salads.

He sighed and said, "How're things at the college? Are you really concerned you might lose your job?"

"Your turn to switch the subject, eh?" We shared a smile. "Things are okay. Being at a private school has its ups and downs. Up with the economy and down with it too. My assistant is wrapping up my three classes on Women in the Wild West, 1865–1885; The Spanish Influence on the Southwest, Seventeenth and Eighteenth Centuries; and Women in the Twentieth Century. Oh, and I'm researching the life of Julia Cameron, the nineteenth-century photographer."

His smile told me he did know of her. He loved history almost as much as I. It was part of his fascination with Alzheimer's. A lifetime of history hidden just beneath the surface of his patients' silent lips. *Shared interests and all that...*

"What are you going to do with your research?" Dane leaned forward. "The look on your face tells me it's not just another class syllabus."

I rubbed the sweat off the outside of my goblet. "Thinking about a book."

"It's about time."

Surprised by his reaction, I quickly looked up at him. "You think I could do it?"

"You can do anything."

His naked admiration made me want to shrink off my chair and hide under the table. How insane was I to accept this invitation to dinner? To consider his invitation to a dance? One dance with him and it would be all over. Again.

1978

Newly arrived from Santa Fe, Dane McConnell already knew many of the old dances. His mother wanted him to keep up with his dancing, so he came to my mother's studio one afternoon. I eyed him shyly; Mother boldly looked him over. He was a young man by then, sinewy and muscled from a summer's ranch work—an uncle's ranch, he told me. He held me like a professional when we danced. Even Miguel could not hold a candle to this one, I thought. And instantly I was falling.

Mother was often acting odd these days, occasionally getting lost and then angry at me as if I had misplaced her myself, but that day in the studio, I felt downright uncomfortable. At one point she roughly pulled me aside and took my place in Dane's arms, ostensibly to show me how to do the steps right. But I had done the steps correctly—I was sure of it. Dane glanced at me in confusion but obediently kept up with his new partner. In a minute he relaxed with the music and kept pace with Mother, seeing it as a challenge more than an intrusion.

Meanwhile I was in the corner, watching, watching. Mother never said a word to me, never looked my way again that day, intent only on her new student.

Was she jealous of me? Jealous that a boy might look at me, might want to hold me instead of her? She had been unaccountably clingy of late, pulling me close for impromptu hugs, when before, we had gone months without an embrace. I was torn between the pleasure of a mother who seemed to want me again and the displeasure of a mother who was suddenly too close. She seemed to need the physical reminders of who she was. Something was shifting deep inside her. I just could not figure out what.

She was forgetting, forgetting, always forgetting lately. Many of her students had quit, leaving just six of us now. I had heard one mother sigh in disgust over the phone when I said she wasn't home; Mother had missed another scheduled appointment.

Worse, I knew where she was. At the bar. More and more she seemed to be at the bar. And when she wasn't, she often retreated to her dark bedroom again.

So that day, when she danced with Dane, I allowed it without complaint. It was good to see her remembering the steps, enjoying herself in the dance, living without benefit of alcohol or men in a bar. I could see that Dane was still glancing my way when Mother wasn't looking. I could allow this.

And later I would dance with Dane McConnell all by myself. It was all in how you played it, life. These days I was playing it smart. I had to, if Mother and I were going to survive.

C H A P T E R   S I X

December 17

Mother had always had a wandering eye. As the '50s edged toward the '60s, as Taos lost some of its romantic edge, she went to school, got her nursing degree, and signed up as an army nurse. My mother and nursing seemed like an odd mix, but in a year that Marilyn Monroe and Arthur Miller found love, I supposed there were stranger combinations.

The year 1957 was a time of change. Ed Sullivan vowed to never have Elvis Presley's vulgar performance on his television show, then later paid him $50,000 for three appearances. The USSR's *Sputnik I* and *II* were launched into orbit while the USA's rocket blew up on the launching pad. Philip Morris changed its famous brown packaging on its cigarettes to make it more appealing on color television, and things like whiskey-flavored toothpaste briefly entered the market.

My mother was ready to go to war. Her dance studio fumbled along for a few years, but without her backbone, it was just so much limp flesh. Mothers stopped calling, and classes grew spare. People were more interested in rock-'n'-roll than the old Spanish folk dances. Mother always could sense change on the wind. She probably saw her change in vocation as a preemptive strike.

Yet she didn't sell her little house with the connecting studio. Sure, the studio became a storage unit, but she could have sold it. She cleared it out for those years when I was in junior high and high school. Taught us the old, hypnotic, gypsy ways of dance—but never sold the old place. Maybe she wanted it around as a fall-back if her new plans didn't come to fruition. She eventually came back to Taos to raise me; it seemed everybody always came back to this place. But for a time she was a sojourner in a far land.

Her entry from 1957:

Part of me wants to know what Gordon knew in this part of the world. To understand what it is to be far from home and all one holds dear, especially at Christmastime. There is little laughter and no snow out this way, just damp cold. The notoriety I sought in leaving New Mexico under the army's banner has quickly lost its luster. There is little adventure to be had here. My hours are long, the pay slim, the work dull. We are not at war, and if we were, I'm sure I'd be far from it. If the Cold War continues, there will be action soon, someplace.

The only bright light in all of this is that I've met a man. Marcellin Mongeau. As a part of the French press corps, he is in

the region reporting on the recovery of the Korean people and her
government. A tangle with a bicycle landed him on our ward.
As soon as I saw him I knew he and I would be spending some
time together.

    Perhaps this Christmas will bring me some laughter after all.

My eyes ran over his name again. Marcellin Mongeau. My
father. Better known as Marc than Marcellin, he had disappeared
years ago. I knew this because I had tried to find him when I was
about twenty. When Mother got so bad; when I felt more lost than
ever. One of those stupid escapades when a searching daughter
looks for a long-lost parent, thinking she'll find herself when she
finds him. I had to learn the hard way that the only way I was going
to find myself was to look within, and through the eyes of Jesus
when I did.

As I read the journal entry and my heart skipped a beat, I knew
there was still work to do on the subject of Dear Old Dad. Still my
eyes searched the room until they landed on the beribboned stack
of letters. They certainly contained Marc's love letters as well as
Gordon's. Did I dare go there? To understand more fully how
Mother had loved? And lost?

Annie, the RN on Mother's ward, ducked her head in. "Hi. If
I'm not interrupting, I thought we'd take Charlotte into the
Christmas room today for a visit." She turned to Charlotte and
gently touched her arm, speaking as if Mother were coherent. "I
bet you'd like that, huh, Charlotte? A little visit to the Christmas
room?"

"Oh," I said, a bit befuddled. "I thought... Is it safe? To move her?"

Annie's kind eyes searched mine. She tilted her head to the side and said, "Charlotte's got little time left. Why not try to give her some enjoyment? We've been taking her out there every other day or so. But it's up to you, of course."

I felt foolish questioning her. She was right. What did it matter if Mother died en route to the Christmas room? She was due to die at any moment. Besides, I was curious to witness her reaction to the carols, to see for myself if she would sing. She had not said one word to me since I arrived, hadn't even looked my way. I thought it highly unlikely.

"You're right," I said finally. "It would be good to give her a change of pace."

Annie looked down the hall and gestured toward the aide at the desk. In seconds they were both in the room, preparing Mother for transport, temporarily removing her IV to leave it behind. "How long will we be down there?" I asked.

"Depends on you and Charlotte. She could stay for the afternoon if she'd like. Sometimes it takes awhile for the music and surroundings to sink in."

I grabbed the stack of letters. "Okay. All set?"

"All set," Annie said, pulling the hospital bed out the door.

"Can I do anything?" I asked meekly.

"No thanks. Just stay behind me," the aide said. What was her name, Joan? I couldn't remember. I had always been lousy with names. My mind briefly leapt to Alz as the reason, but I quickly cast the thought away.

We walked down Main Street and hung a left into the Christmas room. For Advent, Dane had hired a trio of instrumentalists to come and play two hours a day, midmorning, when they were less in demand in other areas of town. The aide pulled Mother to a stop near them and next to a couple of pine-colored twill couches and easy chairs. I sank into one of them, watching as she tended to Mother. Then, with a quick smile for me, she left Charlotte's side to return to her wing. Another aide was at a corner station, patiently conversing with a man insisting he had to go Christmas shopping right away. "I have no presents! I have no presents for the children!"

"Sure you do, Frank," the kind-faced caregiver responded. He guided Frank over to the tree and waved over the large number of bags. "There they all are, every last one of them."

My eyes left Frank and hovered over the five other patients in the room, three of them mobile. The instrumentalists—a cellist, a violinist, and a flutist—were playing "Jesu, Joy of Man's Desiring." It was lovely. My eyes searched Mother's face to see if there was a reaction. Nothing.

Next they played "I Saw Three Ships" and then "Angels from the Realms of Glory." I sat and stared at the chili lights and the gray skies outside. It was snow weather, as my Opa used to call it. Not too cold, not too warm. Lots of moisture in the clouds.

My eyes were drawn back to a distinguished-looking patient

who paced the front. All of a sudden he turned toward Mother and was heading our way. Another woman stood directly before the instrumentalists, swaying in time to their music. The fourth mobile patient was on the small stage, singing as if part of a choir, sometimes keeping pace with the musicians, sometimes not.

The dignified gentleman neared Charlotte and studied her face, never glancing my way. I looked around for help and with some relief saw that the aide in the corner was warily watching it all too. "Name's Wally. Wally tends to think Charlotte's his wife," the male nurse said easily, his eyes still on the man. "Never does her any harm."

I still watched as Wally took my mother's hand in his and gazed at her lovingly. "Marge, you're not looking well, dear heart. Have you not been eating?"

"I think she had breakfast," I said calmly.

"Did she eat much?" Wally asked, stroking Charlotte's forehead.

"Eggs and bacon. A couple of biscuits. A farmer's breakfast," I lied—appeasement therapy, rather.

Relief flooded his face. "Keep eating like that, my dear, and you'll be up and about in no time." "Lo, How a Rose E're Blooming" filled the air, and Wally's eyes left Charlotte's face. He wandered off, leaving her hand dangling at her side.

I rose and walked around the hospital bed, took my mother's cold hand, and placed it under the sheet and blanket. I looked over my shoulder toward Wally, now walking the perimeter of the room, muttering to himself, while three more patients were escorted in. His departure made me feel a little sorry for my mother. Another suitor so easily distracted.

The three newbies seemed content to sit in their wheelchairs and listen. Two of them sang along, doing better than the one on stage. Still no peep from Mother. My eyes followed Wally, wondering who he had been, what he had been like once. He seemed kind, loving. Had Mother ever known such a love from a man?

Wearily I pulled at the pink ribbon and let the letters fan out on my lap. Postmarks from all over the world to three addresses— Korea, England, and New Mexico. All with *MM* in the return address corner. None from Gordon, as I'd expected. Only these from Dear Old Dad. Sent during the years she was stationed in Korea as an army nurse, then later when he was still roaming the globe as a reporter after she had come home.

I let a deep breath slowly escape from blowfish-like cheeks. *Here we go.* Again I felt voyeuristic, reading these words of passion and presence. But I felt as if I had a right to these letters, since my father had never bothered to write to me. Through them I might understand at last how Mother could have loved the blackguard and a little of my own genetic makeup as well. I might not have discovered a sense of self in knowing Marcellin, but I could find out if, say, I might be predisposed to cancer or high blood pressure or diabetes. That was what I told myself anyway.

My Spanish beauty...

I immediately set down the first letter. *Oh, brother.* I could tell it was going to get a little thick. Mother was German through and through. The only thing Spanish about her was her once-long dark hair and her love of *bailadores de España.* With a quick glance at my mother's closed eyes, I cleared my throat and tried again.

My Spanish beauty… I have spent these past weeks interviewing politicians and celebrities, crossing mountain ranges of dizzying heights and unraveling intriguing scenarios, and yet all I can think of is you. In my dreams, you walk toward me, your hair long and undone in the wind, your haunting, promising eyes on me. From the start it was like that with you. You entered my life and from then on, my heart belonged to you. I had little choice. Nor do I now. My Charlotte, ma chérie.

It is your dancing that lives most in my memory, of how you crossed the field to me, hands on hips, chin in air, shoulders and head telling me you own everyone and everything you cross.

I paused. That was an astute observation. People had always had a weird thing with my mother. A polite deference, a nameless light in their eyes. Fascination. Had she affected everyone that way? Or was it something she practiced, became better at as she aged?

The French and the Spanish have always had a special affinity, a connection that binds us by blood and passion and understanding. Though German by birth, you are Spanish in heart. You and I are meant for each other, ma chérie, and I cannot

wait to come back to Korea to see you again. You have ruined
me, Charlotte Elizabeth Mueller. Nobody but you will ever have
my mind, heart, and soul again.

—Marcellin

Well. The guy had fallen hard for Dear Old Mom. I had to give him that. Expecting a self-involved letter from a distant lover, I was surprised by his utter devotion.

I opened another letter and then another, listening to his constant litany of endearments and praises, as well as stories of what he was covering across Korea and beyond in 1958. On occasion he was sent to interview biggies such as the new French president, de Gaulle, or to China and Tibet to cover monumental stories such as the meeting of Mao Tse-tung and Khrushchev in Peking, to Rome as Pope Pius XII died and Pope John XXIII was elected, to China again as they bombarded Quemoy and Matsu Islands.

I paused and stared at Mother wearily sucking in air through the muck that plagued her lungs, holding it for a second, and then releasing it. It was work, this life. It had always been work for her in a way. Had she been more relaxed, free, excited about it all during her years with my father?

His words, his work troubled me. What was it?

Then it struck me. Marcellin loved politics, unraveling the story, as surely as I loved history. I always wanted to know what made people do the things they did throughout history—to understand the gumption of an eighteen-year-old hopping a ship to a land he knew nothing about; the inner strength of a woman on the Oregon trail burying a beloved child; the pleasure of building a home from logs felled from one's own land… Had I inherited this fascination from my father?

I read on.

No one anticipated the Seventh Fleet supplying Quemoy. You Americans do love to be Lone Rangers, don't you? I fear you near another war if you are not careful. For now the Chinese have agreed to hold their fire, but it will not be long until she tucks these errant children back under her skirts.

What had it been like to live through such times? To tangle with mammoth countries like China? By 1956 it was known that the communist government was killing thousands of peasants who resisted the red tide. By 1960 it was estimated that more than twenty-six million people had been executed. Even with terrorists afoot worldwide, I had a hard time identifying.

I recalled that the army reassigned Mother to Washington, D.C., in 1959, which probably suited her rogue boyfriend well. More and more the man seemed to be covering politicians and frequently traveled to D.C. He was there when Castro visited and was warmly received but then was off to cover the Tibetan Kamba tribes fighting the Chinese, the Israeli cargo conflict on the Suez, the monkeys who came back to Earth after orbit, the Chinese seizure of Indian territory, Laos's request of the U.S. to aid against North Vietnam aggression… I could see where things were going. It didn't take my Ph.D. in history to figure out that Mother and my father were going to spend quite a bit of time apart in the coming years. The world was literally exploding with power and correspondingly pulling apart. Russia, France, and China all tried out their new A-bombs by 1964. But I was getting ahead of myself; I eased back into the letters.

At some point an aide brought me a sandwich and another checked Mother's heart monitor. Many of the patients left the Christmas room with the musicians, but I liked the feel of the large room, the quiet Christmas carols playing over the loudspeakers. It gave me a sense of space when I was in the midst of entering the very small recesses of my mother's and father's hearts.

They had been totally immersed in each other, it seemed. From what Marcellin wrote, Mother had given him as much as he had given her. He was crazy about her, and their visits together were obviously passionate, fever-pitched. It was a wonder I hadn't been born then.

I fell asleep in that cozy chair next to Mother and slept as I hadn't in weeks. I dreamed vivid, Technicolor dreams. I could see Marcellin and Charlotte walking hand in hand, stealing kisses at the Lincoln Memorial, him steadying her as she walked along the border of the Washington Memorial Pool. Watching the nation's Christmas tree alight with thousands of bulbs. I could see her smile and could almost see his as well. His words had made him come alive to me, more than a mythic creature, a living, breathing, Charlotte-loving man.

"Krista. Kristabelle." The words came from far off, and I struggled to ascertain their origination.

"Krista!"

I awoke with a start then to find Dane beside me, on his knees. He was smiling, and I smiled back sheepishly. Falling asleep in a public place was not my best habit. Had I been snoring? Sleeping with my mouth hanging open?

"Needed a little siesta, did you?"

"It was just so nice," I said sleepily. "So warm, so comforting with the Christmas music playing."

"I want to show you something," he said, taking my hand and gently pulling me up.

"What? What is it?" I asked, glancing back at Mother.

"She's fine. The aide will keep an eye on her, won't you, Jack?"

"Will do, boss."

He pulled me out the door and into the entry and then toward the front door. It was growing dark, I noticed for the first time. How long had I been reading? Sleeping?

"Close your eyes," he said, moving behind me to cover them. I didn't know what I liked more—the element of surprise or the feel of him behind me, almost holding me with his elbows over my shoulders and his long, warm fingers gently over my brows.

"Dane…," I pretended to whine. I had to at least keep up appearances.

"Kristabelle." I could smell it before he lifted his hands, could feel the quick, cold pricks on my cheeks.

"Snow," I breathed. We walked to the top of the berm, and Dane brushed off the concrete bench there. Big, fat flakes filtered down about us. I held out my hand to glimpse the crystalline, fleeting beauty of a few even as they melted on the heat of my skin, before joining Dane on the bench. He held out a friendly, non-threatening hand, and I took it, content to share this moment of appreciation.

I always did like holding hands with Dane McConnell.

The snow continued to come down in great, swillowing clouds, as though God were unloading pillowcases full of goose feathers. The mountains were skirted in gray, with just their bare legs in view. But I loved the contrasts of the earth's red tones and the green sage, the scent of crackling cedar in a neighbor's wood-burning stove mixing with the clean, cold aroma of snow. Dane knew this. It was just one of many things he knew about me.

I grinned as I hadn't for years. Had Mother and my father known this kind of connection?

I could feel Dane's stare on the right side of my face and let my fading grin spread again. It felt good to be admired, so good to fall back into things with Dane. Why couldn't we ever just let ourselves fall for good? My smile grew into a melancholy, wistful sigh that matched my heart.

I dared to look over at him, letting my eyes trail from our entwined hands, up his arm to his eyes, so solemn, so intent on mine.

"I know, Kristabelle," he whispered. He raised my hand to his lips and gently kissed each of my knuckles—slowly, ever so slowly—his eyes on mine, then back on the landscape before us. "I know. Just let it be awhile, will you?"

I didn't answer, and he obviously took my silence as agreement.

"You're getting fat," Mother told me as she zipped up the back of my dress.

I frowned at my image in the mirror. I had wondered the same thing. Over and over I had wondered. But Mother was hardly a great judge of anything these days. Elena said I looked beautiful, but the more I dated Dane McConnell, the more cold Mother seemed to be. She had given up on her studio, on life, it seemed to me, only keeping up with lessons for Dane and me out of a sense of pride.

I elected to ignore her comment. It burned, her words, but she was drunk and couldn't remember what I kept telling her, that Dane and I were going to the movies. She was rail-thin herself, electing to smoke and drink rather than eat. I didn't think I was that fat. I'd gained a few pounds in the last months, going out with Dane all the time, but I kind of liked how I looked.

"Only one thing a boy wants," she said, looking over my shoulder and meeting my eyes in the mirror. "One thing."

"Not Dane. He's not like that."

She snorted in derision.

"Yes, Mother. You would know, wouldn't you? You would know what the boys want." I turned to face her, my fury growing. "You think

I can't hear you at night? You think I don't see those guys sneaking out in the morning? You call yourself a Christian! You don't know the first thing about morals or what good guys want—"

She slapped me then. The sound seemed to come from somewhere else. The sting on my cheek followed three seconds later. For a suspended moment we did nothing but stare at each other in horror, in shock, in anger.

Her hand went to her lips, sorrow filling her blue eyes, so like my own. But I was sure there was nothing but hatred in mine. I hated her, hated her with everything in me. She was mean. Why did she have to be so mean? And now she had hit me.

I glared at her, loathing the sight, the smell, the feel of her presence.

"Don't say it, Krista. Don't say it."

She knew it then, my hatred.

"You won't ever be able to take it back. It will sit here, between us forever."

"Like you slapping me?" I spat out. I started to cry because it hurt, ached, to hate her so. It tore at my heart, made me feel all crumbly inside. I heard Dane pull up outside and turned away before I could say what I wanted to, what she asked me not to say. Before my aching heart collapsed and I couldn't stop myself from unloading the black pain.

"Krista— I…"

But I ran.

Chapter Seven

December 18

The letters and Marc and Charlotte's romance apparently stopped for a couple of years in the early sixties. There was some indication that she took up with a black man; leaflets from rallies and demonstrations, as well as a few brief notes, made me wonder. I didn't know his name. But it was like Mother to take up with a man of a different color, more for the sake of shaking up Oma and Opa than for any genuine devotion. Perhaps Marc had hurt her or the distance had gotten the better of them. Maybe, as with Dane and me, they just could never get it together and stay together.

One happy conclusion Mother came to was that the only man who guaranteed he'd never leave her was Jesus. In 1962 beneath the hymn "Christians, Awake," she wrote this:

I am back in the Far East again, this time in Vietnam. I'm pre-pared to see Marcellin any day now. This is his beat, and it's only a matter of time until our paths cross. It's been two years since I've heard from him, but I still long for his voice, his touch. No man has ever moved me as Marc did once. Gordon came close, but even he wasn't Marcellin.

Other than Christ, that is. I've found that I must remain a believer since no other God would have me. How can I deny a man who would die for me, forgive me my transgressions? I know that might sound self-serving, but I cannot deny what I am. Perhaps one day I will serve others as I see the women around me do. For now I accept who I am as God accepts me and hope that one day I will be more.

I could fill the following years with well-known history. In '63 Ngo Dinh Diem was assassinated in South Vietnam, followed by JFK's assassination and, in turn, Lee Harvey Oswald's murder. In '64 a U.S. destroyer was attacked in the Gulf of Tonkin, and America retaliated with bombs over North Vietnam. Mother's presence in the region before this told me what I had already guessed, that the United States had been preparing for intervention in the Vietnamese struggle. I sighed. Everyone knew how that would turn out.

In the meantime I knew that 1962 was the year Mother turned forty. Had she been as reluctant as I was to hit the big 4-0? I had always prided myself in embracing my age, celebrating the passing years instead of hiding them. But turning thirty-seven had changed something within me. I was asking myself all the questions that the media had pushed at me: Would I ever find love? marriage? have children of my own? The years had flowed past me like a flash flood in a gully, leaving debris and damage and struggling, struggling, always struggling new life. I continually thought of my life as "Next year I'll…" and the following year found myself saying the same things.

A pang of empathy went through me as I looked at Mother and imagined her in Vietnam observing America on the brink of war and her own heart on the brink as well. Anticipating Marc's arrival, she must've felt as I did when I neared Dane McConnell. She knew she shouldn't fall back with him, just as surely as I knew I shouldn't with Dane. Their jobs would keep them apart just as surely as Dane's and mine kept us apart.

Okay, I knew it was a shallow excuse. But at least I had an excuse.

I wonder if Mother had thought it through that far. Judging from her note, I think she was merely excited about seeing him again, longing for him, not preparing her heart to repel the man who could hurt her. As I did. I paged through the book of carols but found no other notations from that year. A search through the storage unit had given me no clues either. I just had to assume that they got back together in '62 or '63. I was born in '65, and though I never took my father's last name, it was Mongeau on my birth certificate.

A part of me wanted to reach out and warn her, to tell her not to do it, to refuse his advances. A part of me was glad she had fallen for him and been hurt. I was not proud of this, but it felt like justice. Mother had never been the kind of mom I always longed for. What kind of mother left her six-year-old to fend for herself? I remembered making jelly sandwiches and chocolate milk because Mother couldn't get out of bed. Forget about nutrition or a balanced diet. Mother only cared about me when it reflected back on her. If I got less than an A on a report card, I was in trouble. If I forgot a step with my dance troupe, she went on and on about it.

Looking back, I realize Mother probably had some chemical imbalance. Had they known what they know today, they might have prescribed Zoloft, and I might have had Insta-Mom. But at the time, all I knew was that I had no daddy, a mother who was incapacitated much of the time, and lots of friends who had two loving parents. I was alone for all intents and purposes. Only my Oma and Opa and Elena gave me a sense of balance, love, and foundation. Without them, I knew I would have been much more of a basket case than I already was. I'd paid my dues in dollars spent on therapy. I didn't need any more issues in my life beyond what I couldn't seem to settle with Mother. I was glad for what I had had. Really.

Only problem was that by the time Oma and Opa were gone and it was just us, Mother and me, I didn't feel it was enough, and she clearly felt the same. Elena was our only reprieve from each other. And here we sat, thirty years later, still just the two of us.

Maybe I had been wrong to keep Dane at arm's length. Maybe I had been foolish all this time. It would be nice to have another in our midst, a leavening force. But I couldn't bring myself to use him as such. If I came to Dane, I had to be ready to give my whole heart. I just didn't know if my heart would ever be intact enough to do so.

I was staring out Mother's window, against the glare of a bright winter sun on the white landscape—it had snowed all night— when the doctor arrived.

"Heard she wasn't doing well today," Suzanne said.

I turned around, watching her move from monitor to patient, put on her stethoscope, and lean over to listen to what I could hear from here—Mother laboring to breathe. She was swollen, so swollen, her whole body now filling with fluid.

Suzanne rose, took the stethoscope from her ears, and wrapped it in a neat coil before slipping it in her jacket pocket. "You sure you don't want her in the hospital?"

"I thought you said it wouldn't make much difference."

"No. But it might buy you some peace of mind."

"From what I can tell, the staff here is giving her about as much attention as she could get. As long as she isn't in pain, as long as you can do for her here what you could do for her there, I'm all right with it."

Suzanne studied me. "Okay. I'm going to call hospice and have them send someone out to talk with you each day."

"To me? I don't need anyone to talk to."

She gave me a sad smile. "Everyone needs someone."

"Well, I'm fine. I've spent a wad on a therapist who's helped me get ready for this day." Almost ready. I knew there were things that remained unresolved with Mother, things that would probably remain forever unresolved. "And I have...friends," I said lamely. I had almost said Dane, thinking of him and Elena. Suzanne lifted her cell phone after a moment. "Anytime, Krista, that you need me or your mom needs me, call. Or if you change your mind about hospice. Okay?"

So this was the look that doctors gave people about to lose a parent. A shiver ran down my back. I wasn't ready. For whatever reason, I just wasn't. Mother couldn't die. Yet.

I turned to stare at Mother as the doctor left the room. What did I want from her? What did I need? She wasn't physically or mentally able to give me anything that I had craved since childhood. I let out a sound of exasperation, then shook my head. Maybe I did need someone to talk to.

Elena.

Turning to the CD player by Mother's bed, I pressed Play, and Nat King Cole's smooth voice filled the air. "There's your music, Mother. I'll be back." I bent to dutifully kiss her forehead and quickly left the room.

When I took a deep breath outside of Cimarron, I realized that Mother's room already smelled of death.

My car made fresh tracks in the snow on Elena's road. From the look of it, no one had been in or out since I left that morning. Elena had given me some space since I arrived, hovering just out of my line of vision so I would know she was there but never so close

I felt smothered. She knew I'd back away if she did. Elena knew everything about me. Almost.

I slid and fishtailed here and there as my Prelude made its way through the dense, wet drifts, but I never got stuck. She opened the door, obviously having heard my engine, and smiled and waved, wiping her hands on an apron as old as I. She waved me in, as if half expecting me not to come in on my own.

"Since I was snowed in, I thought I'd make some tamales," she said with a grin.

Elena never drove in snow, even if it was just a dusting. I didn't question it; the woman was seventy-something years old. I figured it was her prerogative. The kitchen smelled wonderful as aromas of corn and oil and pork filled the air. Elena had always made the best tamales, adding *carnitas,* tender, braised pork, to the corn stuffing. She served them warm, with a lovely dark sauce that I always referred to as Mexican gravy.

"Hungry?" she asked.

"Always, at your house."

She gestured toward the bar, and I gratefully took a tall stool, my mouth already watering. Elena was methodical about things, and so I prepared my stomach to wait. Sure enough, first came the iced water, poured into a tall Mexican glass with a blue rim and bubbles in the walls. Then the knife, fork, and spoon, with cloth napkin. At last she set the tamale on the plate and poured the thick sauce over it.

"M'm," I said appreciatively with waggling brows, immediately setting to slicing open the cornhusk and letting the insides steam for a moment before taking a mouth-scalding bite. I couldn't help it. I always managed to scald my mouth, so eager was I to sample Elena's tamales.

"H-hot," I said, taking a gulp of water.

"But good, no?" she asked, repeating our lines that we had said countless times a year for as long as I could remember.

"Good, good, yes. Best ever." I always told Elena they were the best ever.

And as expected, she smiled in satisfaction.

"Are you taking some over to Robbie?" I asked, shoveling another bite in my mouth. Robbie was Elena's grown son, slightly older than I. He was divorced, which greatly grieved his mother. Two younger sons had moved to Albuquerque.

"I am. He'll have the kids tonight, and I wanted them to have some of their grandmother's world-famous tamales. That girl"—Elena consistently referred to Robbie's ex as "that girl"—"never cooks. Can you imagine?"

I frowned in what I hoped was an empathetic and yet noncommittal expression. Never mind that I rarely cooked myself.

She turned away and then came back to me, already offering me more to eat. "Maybe you'd like to take them to him?" she asked too casually.

"Elena...," I said in warning. She had always wanted me to marry either Dane or Robbie.

"Ah, so your heart still belongs to Dane."

"*Elena.*"

"Okay, okay," she said, raising her hands and ducking her

head. "I cannot help it if my Lord and Savior, Jesus Christ, who sits at the right hand of the Father, leads me to speak the truth."

I gave her a knowing smile. She always resorted to Jesus when she needed an out. Who could argue with her when she did? "Tell me how Robbie is doing," I said.

As she filled me in on the latest happenings in her son's life, I shoveled down the rest of the tamale, then half the glass of water in a vain attempt to assuage my burning tongue. I had never felt much of a connection with Robbie other than a vague sense of familial loyalty. We didn't really have anything in common other than our love of Elena. Before she could get back to the suggestion that maybe Robbie and I could get together while I was home, I rose and walked to her old loom. I had always loved the feel of the rough-hewn pine, the thick, stiff, desert-colored yarns Elena wove with.

The loom had been built by Elena's great-grandfather. It wasn't vertical, like the traditional Navajo looms, but horizontal, taking up a five-by-five-foot space. It was perfect in this pure New Mexican setting down to the very floors of Elena's house, which were of hardened mud, similar to adobe brick.

The floor was a traditional oxblood clay, which actually used one part blood to five parts water, a shovel full of ashes, and enough dirt to make it spreadable. The blood made it more durable because of a chemical reaction with the ash, and it made the floor a deep cordovan red. Then it had been polished with river stones. While I could never see myself mixing up a batch of blood and mud, I had always loved the authentic feel of it. Paired with lovely century-old handwoven textiles on the walls, done in the Rio Grande, Rio

Grande Saltillo, and Vallero styles, it made me feel as though I were in a warm, cozy, inviting museum rather than someone's home.

Above me, *latillas,* stripped baby aspen branches, were set in a herringbone pattern across *vegas,* long posts across the ceiling. It reminded me of the forts we used to make as children, lean-tos that sheltered us against a summer's afternoon storm. To my right, an old *baúl,* or chest, had folded *bancos* on top of it, as in the old days. The blankets had always been placed on the bench during the day and used for warmth come nighttime, when one wasn't huddled next to a *fogón,* letting the fire's heat seep into chilled bones. Yes, being at Doña Elena's house always made me feel as though I were entering a more gentle time in Taos history. I loved it.

"May I?" I asked, picking up the wooden shuttle.

She nodded her assent, a tamale on a plate in one hand, a fork in the other. She watched me as I wove through the reeds. Elena had dyed all the yarns in the weaving herself as her ancestors had done prior to the arrival of synthetic dyes in 1860. She prided herself on the authenticity of her craft and seemed to relish the work, as if she could reach out to her great-great-great-grandmother while she steeped imported Mexican brazilwood to create the red-purple, or the root of the madder plant for when she desired a more orange tinge to her reds. *Chamisa,* rabbit brush, and *cota,* Navajo tea, surrendered lovely yellows. It was the bindweed and snakeweed that produced yellow-greens, or she would use yellow dye over indigo to produce a true green. The *churro* wool felt raw and rough and reassuring under my fingers, and the reeds reminded me of the instrumentalists in Dane's Christmas room. Except these reeds wielded a different kind of magic. It only took a few minutes until I remembered the rhythm of this dance, felt the satisfaction of a completed row.

Elena finished her tamale and joined me at the loom, following behind to tightly tuck each woven strand next to its neighbor. We wove in silence for some time, content in the work. An hour turned into two before I paused for a sip of water and to look at my adopted grandmother. "Elena, did my mother ever help you in your weavings?"

"No." Elena took the shuttle from my hand and wound a new, maize-colored yarn around the base, preparing to introduce the new color. "She claimed she was never good at anything but dance. I knew better, but I could never persuade her to try. Not so, her daughter."

I nodded, reaching to gently touch the taut weaving, studying the waves that reminded me of the plains full of sagebrush. Elena had told me that decades ago there had been no sage. It was only after the shepherds arrived and the sheep overgrazed the prairies, that the invasive brush took over. "Would she come and watch you?" I asked casually.

"Often," Elena said, tucking her chin toward her ample bosom. She looked at me as if she were gazing over the top of reading glasses. "You and your mother never understood each other."

"No. We didn't." Elena set to work, and I waited for her to say more. At last I asked, "Did you understand her?"

Elena paused to study the yarns before her, as if concerned a mistake had been made. We both knew there was nothing wrong, but I allowed it, allowed her time to formulate her response. When she settled on it, her brown eyes held mine steady.

"Your mother knew me and loved me, and I, her. There was much that was hurt in that woman from an early time. She was like a prickly pear cactus—showing her gray scars but continuing to grow."

I contemplated her words for a moment. "I thought she just stopped growing when she got hurt."

Elena shook her head. "No, *mi hermanita*. We never stop growing, no matter how much we might want to. Pain might change the direction of our growth, but we keep on as long as we live." She shrugged. "It is the way God made us. Like adobe, one layer after another."

"Or like weavings, row after row, even if an odd color is added."

Elena smiled approvingly and handed me the shuttle again.

"Each weaving is different, much like people. Some have a tighter, stiffer weave, while others hold softer, looser loops. Some weavings wave with the vibrant colors of a Comanche sunset, and still others cling to a more pale, pastel palette."

As I wove through the tense strands, I thought of Mother and what her weaving would be like. I believed that on top it would hold light, promising color, that farther down it would depict the Alzheimer's knots that tied up her mind and memory, the encroaching darkness of life slipping away, the shading of hope dimmed. But I began to spot some curious color in her weaving too, color I would never have imagined there.

It was the letters, the notes, that were working on me, revising my grasp on our shared history, making me give her a little more grace. Making me give her a little more color. A little more light.

"Come," Elena said. "You will take me over to Cimarron now for a visit with your mother."

I glanced up at her kind face and set down the shuttle. "Charlotte would like that."

I sat back and watched Elena humming, chatting to Mother as if they were sharing a good conversation. Most of the staff were careful to include Mother when they talked, sending queries her way that they never expected answered. Dane consistently reminded us that hearing was one of the last senses to go. But Elena talked, really talked to Mother.

She had brought a newly completed weaving and cast it over Mother's slight body. Elena then picked up Charlotte's hands and ran her fingertips over the weave, telling her that we had just been talking about how people were like weavings. She told her about the colors and how this was just like one her great-grandmother had made. She pulled a jar of honey lotion from her bag and rubbed my mother's bony but swollen hands, massaging them.

I turned away then from the intimacy of their friendship, an intimacy I couldn't hope to equal, even as a daughter. I hadn't even noticed my mother's dry skin until Elena began working on it. I hadn't thought to sit and talk as she was doing now. If Mother was coherent, just unable to speak, her life had become a nightmare.

And just then I felt the loneliest, darkest pang of sorrow for another human being I'd ever experienced.

We sang the words to "Blue Christmas" at the top of our lungs as we walked toward the Rio Grande Gorge Bridge that night, five teens bent on getting high on life instead of drugs. I flirted with Julian with his stringy hair and wannabe-hippie ways, then Louis, whom we always referred to as Farmboy. They were nice kids, good kids, from Dane's youth group. For the first time in my life, I felt a part of something. Going to church, getting to know them, it had been the best. Except none of them knew. None of them knew what had happened to me...

I ran up to Farmboy and leaped onto his back for a piggyback ride, smiling back at Blair, the other girl in our small circle of friends, and then Dane, always Dane. Dane and I hadn't been getting along very well since...for the last few weeks. He looked kind of sick as he watched me with Farmboy, but I quickly looked away. We reached the center of the bridge and lay down on the sidewalk, gazing up at stars and moon and satellites, feeling the chill of the winter-cold cement on our backs. We waited and waited for the trucks to come by. Eighteen-wheelin', we called it, thrilling to the rumble that shook us into heaves of laughter every time a huge truck passed by. When the third one had passed, I rose and looked over the edge, down to the roiling dark waters, shimmering in the moon-light. I stared and stared, then began walking back toward Dane's car.

He was behind me; I could sense it. Wanting to reach out and touch me... I decided then, on a whim. We were almost off the bridge; the cliff was not ten feet away. But when I climbed up and perched on the top rail of the bridge, a thousand feet above the Rio Grande, teetering back and forth with a nervous giggle, Blair screamed, and I got nervous.

Julian told me to get off. Farmboy shouted.

I walked on, determined to make it, determined to choose a course all my own. I jumped off at the end, proud of myself for making it, surprised to find myself trembling. I looked around at my mute friends.

But it was Dane's face I settled on. Confusion. Fear. Anger. Mostly confusion.

"What is going on, Krista?" he said, clearly wanting to yell at me but keeping his voice under tight control. "Why would you do that?"

"What?" I shrugged. "That? I just wanted to see, to see if I could. Let's go home."

Dane shook his head, ran a hand through his hair in frustration. "You honestly don't see why that could be bad? You could have killed yourself!"

"Get off my back, Dane. What's life if you don't live it?"

"Death," he said. "You're talking about the line between life and death. Don't ever do something like that again."

"Maybe I will; maybe I won't."

Chapter Eight

December 19

It was unclear how in '62 my mother and father did meet again, but I did know they fell right back into a relationship. The letters arrived sparingly between 1962 and 1964, presumably because they were together more. But by the time I was born in '65, my dad was largely AWOL. When I was about three months old, Mother broke her tradition of writing only every five years and wrote this under "Blue Christmas":

> *Krista was born this year, and her birth is the only brightness in my world. She has her father's perfectly proportioned lips, his nose, his hair. Every time I look at her I miss Marcellin. He is still traveling the world covering one story after another while I am considered officially discharged from the military. A part of me is relieved to be done with service, done with blood and*

*death and war. A part of me aches to be there to help wrap
things up and bring our boys home. LBJ has offered peace and
ceased bombing; this dreadful war has gone on long enough.
Leaving before the troops makes me feel as though I didn't finish
my job, but I pray that it is indeed over. It seems we have our
own wars to fight here, with Watts erupting in riots and peace
marches that seem to demean what we were trying to accomplish
over there. I laugh at myself. Had I not joined the army as a
nurse, seen for myself what was going on, I probably would be
marching along with the flower-power gals.*

*I have returned to Taos to be near my parents since Marc is
gone so often. They delight in their granddaughter, and I believe
my mother has almost forgiven me for eloping with Marcellin. I
never was one who wanted the big wedding. For as much as I
adore dancing and celebration, I abhor pomp and tradition,
and given our few days together halfway around the world, we
had little choice. Now here I am. A new mother in her forties.
Alone. Who would have guessed?*

At the end of '65, it might have seemed like the war in Vietnam
was coming to an end. At the time we'd only lost about 1,300 men.
But the following year things escalated, and we lost another 5,000.
For my mother's sake, I was glad she hadn't remained in the military.
Certainly anything she saw before her departure paled in comparison to what was to come. So many men, American and Vietnamese,
dead. Somewhere around 750,000 by the end of 1971, 46,000 of
them American, with far more wounded.

A part of me wished that my father had died then. I know that sounds awful, but it would have been easier for my mother and me to accept if we could have mourned his death and been done with it. Instead, we spent the next two decades waiting for Marcellin Mongeau to come home.

My eyes ran back over Mother's script. *Krista was born this year, and her birth is the only brightness in my world.* I never knew that I had ever brought Mother comfort or light or joy. I could remember her smiling at me, the sweet surprise I felt at its rarity. Children weren't supposed to be surprised by their mother's joy over them. But I was.

"Hey," Dane said, walking into Mother's room, hands stuffed in his jeans pockets.

"Hey yourself," I returned. I gave him a gentle smile, realizing I'd missed him. "Feel like going for a drive?" he said, staring absently at Mother's chart. "Charlotte, is it okay with you if I escort your lovely daughter on a drive?"

I looked at Mother, half expecting her to answer. A crazy inclination, since there had been virtually no change in her condition nor any response toward me. I felt helpless, claustrophobic, stifled all of a sudden. I rose. "That would feel really good right now." I reached for my leather coat. "Where are we goin'?"

"I don't know. Alaska or Mexico?" It was an old line. Ever since we were in high school Dane and I had loved to drive. We'd pick up at the drop of a hat and drive for as long as we had gas money to go—and return. We'd pick our direction, north or south, east or west, and just go.

"Let's hit Mexico," I said. Once we'd headed toward Mexico

but stopped at Truth or Consequences—I swear there's a town of that name—and we did the inevitable. Dane chose Truth, and I asked him if he'd ever kissed Blair. He hadn't. I chose Consequences. He made me dance *el vase de los paños*—the handkerchief dance designed for multiple partners—by myself along the side of the road until three truckers came by and honked at my futile efforts. I'll never forget how I smiled and threw my head back in laughter or how, as the sun set in brilliant shades of anthem red and desert pink, he threw in a cassette tape and joined me for a *chotís,* an old two-step.

"We'll just be gone for a couple of hours, Mother," I said, as if she would wave us on and tell us to have a good time. It was contagious, this method of speaking to her as if she could hear. I pulled my hair out of the neck of my jacket and, with a final glance toward Mother, followed Dane out of the room.

"What are you thinking about?" he asked.

"The time when we drove toward Mexico and ended up in Truth or Consequences."

He smiled and ducked his head, then pulled it to the side in a quick gesture of remembrance. His eyes told me he had never forgotten.

"Got enough gas?" I asked, wanting to direct our conversation, not wanting him to ask me about the dance tomorrow night. I still didn't know if I had the guts to meet him in that outfit. Or if it was best. Was I just chicken, or was God trying to tell me to stay away? *Fear is not of the Lord,* Elena always said. So then, was God trying to tell me to go?

We climbed into his car, and he chose the long leisurely route, which wound away from the mountains and past the old *adobe morada,* where priests used to go to confess their sins and beat it out of themselves via flagellation. I looked over my shoulder until it was out of sight, then sat back, staring at the rectangular plots of land we passed by.

"What?" Dane asked, breaking our silence.

"I was just thinking about the adobe morada back there."

"And?"

"Why is that we think we have to beat ourselves up to be penitent? That others have to beat themselves?"

"Is this purely a rhetorical question, or are you getting at something in particular?"

I stared out the window as we climbed out of a verdant little valley and curved around to Highway 150.

"Krista? You still with me?"

"Yes. Just thinking."

He left me alone then to complete my thought process and share when I was ready.

"For years now," I began, "I've wanted Mother to suffer for her sins against me. I thought she deserved something like the adobe morada."

"Ah," he said, still facing forward.

I looked back out my window. At dry grasses peeking out of snow-laden fields and rocks steaming in the sun.

"Not a statement full of grace, I know," I said lowly.

"Sometimes, Krista, we don't feel full of grace. But recognizing our unforgiveness is the first step toward grace."

"Is it like a Twelve-Step program? AA?"

"Yes," he said, playing along, "I think they call it PWNG—People Who Need Grace."

"That'd be pretty much all of us."

"It could be a whole new business for me, hosting PWNG groups at Cimarron. Think of it. We'd be swamped."

"Or we could just go to church every Sunday and let God take care of it."

"There's that idea, too," he said, stifling a grin.

I sighed and looked outside again. "Sometimes I wonder if I'll ever get my act together, Dane."

He reached out then, his hand at the back of my neck. He couldn't look at me, I knew; the road was too winding. But his hand felt good, reassuring. Gentle. I forced myself to concentrate on that aspect, not to move away as I was so inclined. I'd moved away far too long…

"You're getting there, Krista. I can see it in you."

I nodded. "It's all tied up with my mother. I'm just now unraveling it."

It was his turn to nod. He dropped his hand. I could tell he was swallowing an *I told you so*. He had every right to say it. But he didn't. He was that kind of guy.

We were heading west toward the blufflike mesas in the distance, the highway ribboning over hills of sage, the sun filtering through high, thin clouds, the sky the color of blue suede, when I saw the signs for the gorge. "Can we pull over up ahead?"

"Sure," Dane said with a slightly forced tone. He'd never quite forgiven me for that night on the bridge as kids. It was high time the man got over it!

He pulled next to a California RV aptly called the Intruder. Some marketer wasn't thinking when they named that vehicle. Who wanted to ride in an Intruder? To be an intruder? My sense of ownership, of indignation at an innocent tourist's appearance, surprised me. Who was I to claim this place as mine, to desire to keep another out? Wasn't I a registered Colorado voter now?

We stepped up on the sidewalk, Dane behind me, and moved forward. My heart always picked up a little because in a few steps, the cliff gave way to gorge. This was the second deepest gorge in the Southwest, and with five more steps there was nothing but the bridge between me and the Rio Grande below. Kids used to throw things down at rafters that floated the river in summertime. Until rumor had it that someone was killed by a water balloon, it had been going so fast. Now the prank carried a mammoth fine and potential criminal charges should someone get hurt.

I walked to the middle of the bridge and leaned over the rail, looking down at snow-covered banks and the edges of ice where the water didn't flow as fast. The center of the current looked wintry black, still whitecapped in the deepest, fastest areas even though the water was low.

Blowing my cheeks out, I stepped up onto the lower bar of the railing, the better to peer over. I leaned a little farther, wondered if I would ever have the urge to jump, remembering the time I actually walked the top bar. The sense of power, control. The teetering threat of falling, falling—

He came out of nowhere. One second I was looking at the frosty waters a thousand feet below me, the next I was hitting the cement sidewalk. I winced and then groaned, feeling the weight of him on top of me. I gasped for air, tried to make sense of our circumstances.

"*Dane,*" I said, finding my breath at last, "what are you *doing?*" I looked up at him, his face inches from mine.

"Krista...I, uh...I'm sorry." Confusion and embarrassment blazed across his face. He quickly got off me and gave me a hand up. The Californians with the RV, an elderly couple, stared at us like the best of intruders. His hand went nervously from the back of his neck, then out to brush me off.

I indignantly pushed away his hand and stared at him. "Dane." I waited impatiently for an explanation. The Californians moved off, glancing over their shoulders at us as if we were a couple of wild bears that couldn't be trusted.

"Krista, I don't know. I looked over at you, and you were leaning so far over the railing...I, uh... Well, I thought..."

"You thought I was going to *jump?*" I sighed heavily and walked back toward his car.

"Wait. Listen. You were so quiet. I know things have been tough. With your mom and all. With... I was remembering that time you walked the rail." He pulled me to a stop. I half turned but didn't look at him. "It scared me to death that time." He let out a partial laugh. When I glanced at him, I couldn't help the hint of a smile. It *was* a little funny. In an insane kind of way. "I'm sorry," he said, smiling openly now.

I shook my head and let out a scoffing laugh. I wasn't ready to let him entirely off the hook. "Things are hard, Dane, but jumping off the gorge bridge to end it all isn't my idea of how I want to go. I was a stupid kid, *twenty* years ago."

"Right. I know. I'm an idiot. Krista, I'm sorry. Are you all right? Did I hurt you?"

"A little bruised. My shoulder and hip will hurt tomorrow. But no, I'm okay."

He looked so painfully ill at ease, aching to know that all would be okay, so worried about me. So vulnerable.

Stepping forward, I placed my hands on the sides of his face and slowly, tenderly kissed one stubble-covered cheek, then slowly moved to the other. I bent his head forward and pressed my lips to his forehead. I released him a little, and he pulled back an inch, his green eyes searching mine, wild with wonder. I saw his throat bulge as he swallowed hard.

Then he leaned forward, desire flooding his eyes. The old fear returned, fear that he would leave me, though I had always been the one to do the leaving. What was I afraid of? I only knew that Dane surely deserved better, didn't need to adopt my perpetual confusion.

Dane studied me. "What is it you want, Krista? Someone to love you? Someone who won't hurt you as your mother did?"

I made myself stand there, made myself stare back into those green, green eyes. "I don't know… I remember what it was like with you before…when we would dance… I remember, Dane."

I was on the edge. On the brink of discovery. On the precipice and as ready to fall backward as forward. I could barely breathe.

He smiled at me. "The trick to life, I think," he said, "is not only to acknowledge what you are missing but then to go out and make sure it doesn't go missing again."

I wanted to say, *Like missing you.*

He moved in closer, pulling me to him with a hand at my lower back and another to the back of my neck.

I tried to allow it, knowing my rising panic made no sense. But I couldn't help it. "No!" I cried, my voice muffled by his lips.

At once he was backing away, even as I was shoving. "No!" I said, truly angry now, frustrated, unaccountably frightened. I was shaking.

I turned and stumbled away.

"Krista, I'm sorry. Krista, wait. I thought…" His voice turned from confusion to frustration. "What is going on?"

I kept going, making my way to the car, tears blurring my vision. "Krista," he said, pulling me to a stop. His eyes searched my face in consternation. "Krista, are you *frightened* of me?"

"Yes! *Yes.*" I wrenched my arm away from him. "Take me back, Dane. Take me back now."

I was asleep the night it happened. Worn out from a three-hour drama practice, madly preparing for our year-end musical, I was lead dancer in Man of La Mancha. *I got home and found Mother gone. I expected she was on a date. She had been dating William for some time. A part of me was relieved that she could find companionship in someone else.*

Moreover, I was glad they were out of the house. When they were home, William spent as much time watching me as he did my mother. I had turned several times in the last weeks to find him staring at me with a grinning leer. I shivered at the mere thought of him. But if he made Mother happy, I was not going to say a word.

I drank a quick fruit-and-protein milkshake spun in the blender, sped through my homework, took a long, hot shower, and fell into bed. Within moments I was sleeping deeply.

I awakened to find William fumbling, groping me, a ghostly mass in the darkness. He touched me, touched me all over. He covered my mouth with his hands, nearly smothered me as his body and mouth pressed against my flesh.

He told me not to scream, that he would kill me, kill Mother if I did… I felt myself retreat, disappearing behind a wall. Somewhere safe and known…

That was when Elena came in. I don't know how she knew, how she could've guessed, but she went after him like a terrier on a grizzly bear. She screamed and shouted and beat at him with her hands as I had wanted to. But I was afraid, so afraid. It was as if I watched them from a mile away, two tiny creatures in the distance as the sound of sirens drew near.

And then Elena took me into her arms, and I wept, and I knew it was over.

So much was over.

So much ended that night.

CHAPTER NINE

As we neared Cimarron, still wearing our mantle of awkward silence, I finally spoke. "Will you drop me at Elena's?"

"Sure. Krista, I—"

"Please," I said to him sorrowfully. "Believe me, I know this is all about me. I'm trying to get it straight, Dane, I am. And I think I'm close. Just give me a little more time."

He sat back, and I could almost feel him biting his tongue. I sensed the battle within him, the desire to shout in anger, the contortion of will as he tried to maintain his patience just a little longer. I knew he was about to call it quits on this latest effort at something with me. Who would want a woman who didn't want to be kissed? After all this time. After all we had shared.

We had kissed as teens—a couple of times gone to full-blown make-out sessions. But we'd broken up right before that terrible night, and things were never again the same.

I swallowed hard, past the lump in my throat, trying to hold on to my composure. *Just a few more feet...* I coached myself. Dane pulled to a stop. I shook, mumbled an "I'm sorry," and fled from his vehicle. One more second in his presence and I would have burst out crying. He didn't wait for me to get inside. The gravel spun from his tires as he peeled out.

Elena met me at the door. With one look into her kind eyes, I could no longer curb my tears. "I'm so tired, Elena. So tired." Without a word, just an arm around my waist, Elena led me to my bedroom.

"You lie down now, child, and sleep awhile. Tonight I'll make you dinner."

Suddenly weary from the inside out, I sank onto the down comforter with its soft sheen and welcoming fill. It was a small room, painted a prairie tan, the walls hand-plastered. Pine logs crossed the ceiling in an echo of the vegas in the main house. But this room was an add-on, pure contemporary Taos. The bed was of peeled pine too, and all I wanted was to be in it.

I pulled off my jacket and threw it over the corner of the bed.

Elena came in, as I knew she would, with a mug of hot cinnamon tea. She always had a kettle of hot water simmering. She handed me a tissue to dry my tears, still flowing in silent testimony to my misery. "Sleep now," she insisted, putting a hand on my shoulder.

"But my mother—"

"Your mother is the same. I was just there. She'd want you to take this time. It's important, Krista."

"Tonight," I said, almost to myself, "perhaps we can take a sauna." I wanted its soothing warmth. To sit among the cedar planks with the reverent, almost-ceremonial pouring of water from a ladle onto the hot rocks to produce a cloud of steam. I needed to sweat this out, let this darkness find its way out of my heart and soul. Forever.

"Good idea," Elena said. "For now, just sleep."

As soon as she closed the door, I lay down on the perfectly plumped pillow and closed my eyes. There was so much going on in my head I wondered if I could sleep at all. That was the last thing I remembered thinking.

When I awakened, the winter sun was setting to the west among the bluffs of the New Mexican desert. I turned over in bed and watched through my picture window, squinting to observe this evening ritual, cognizant that something inside was shifting. Something monumental.

Deep shadows bent through my room and finally disappeared in a wave of twilight. I sat up and rolled my head in a circle, feeling the tension in my neck and shoulders. I must have been asleep for hours.

After taking a sip of tea, long chilled, I rose and pulled my clothes off. Elena had stopped back in my room at some point, leaving two large, white, Egyptian cotton towels. I wound one around my body and secured it, then tied my long hair in a turban. I felt as though I had checked into a spa.

"Elena?" I called quietly, the echo of my voice bouncing off the large red tiles of the hallway floor. There was no answer.

I padded to the kitchen. There a note waited for me.

Off to get some groceries. Drink your water and take your sauna. We'll talk when I return. E

Beside it was a tall Mexican blue glass, sweating from the melted ice inside. A perfect thin slice of lemon floated on top. I shook my head. Elena always knew how to take care of me.

Obediently I drank the glass of water and then headed down a second hallway to the sauna. It was a tiny room, maybe six feet square, but there were seldom more than two people in it at a time. I closed the door behind me, inhaling the scent of cedar that brought back so many pleasant memories. I settled onto the plank bench next to the stones. I could smell their dry heat.

Bending over, I reached for the cool metal dipper and lowered it into the bucket, then slowly poured the water over the black volcanic stones. As steam rose it sounded like the sizzling rice soup they served at the Chinese restaurant in the Springs. Over and over I did this until a cloud of vapor filled the room from my knees upward. I sat back and inhaled the moisture, my toes wriggling in their relative coolness.

As the steam dissipated, I added more water, and in about half an hour sweat poured nonstop from my skin. I was about to call it quits when Elena appeared in her own towel of white. I smiled,

taking a deep breath of the dry air that entered with her, and gratefully accepted a second cold glass of water.

"The ancients used to sweat until they saw visions. You need to
get some demons out, fine, but no fainting in my sauna."

"No fainting. Got it."

She sat down across from me, leaned her head back, and
sighed. "You are ready?"

"Ready for what?" I said, playing dumb. How did she know?

"Ready to go back and release your foul memories, bury them."

She took my silence as affirmation. "It was God that brought
me to your house that night," she said.

"I know."

"I'm sorry I wasn't there sooner."

I swallowed hard. "I know."

The year of the "incident" Mother's Alz became harder and
harder to deny. On top of her depression, the memory thief had
sneaked into our lives under the radar. She lost her job, her driver's
license, her goals. And the more she lost of her memory, the more
we seemed to see Elena, appearing with food and staying with me
when Mother disappeared. She'd been a faithful friend all my life.

"I didn't know until a few years ago that Alzheimer's plays
tricks on your libido as well as your mind," I said.

Elena nodded, her face shrouded in seriousness. "It wasn't like
your mother to take up with men like that. But as her mind disen-
gaged, her body longed to engage."

"She was a believer, Elena. She knew Jesus then. She knew she couldn't find affirmation in a man, not the way she needed affirmation. I read it. She wrote it down in that Christmas carol book."

Elena sighed, bent to pour water over the stones, then sat back. "We are none of us without sin. We know the way, but it doesn't keep us from straying."

I let that sink in. "Well, yeah, I'm far from perfect myself, but I haven't started picking up men in bars, bringing them home for sex and smokes, and in front of a teenage daughter at that."

Elena paused as if pained. "It hurt you. I'm sorry, child. But no sin is greater than another. We are, all of us, sinners at Jesus' feet."

"I know, cast the first stone and all that. But it was her responsibility, Elena. Her job to see that I was safe. That no one would hurt me. *It was her responsibility.*"

Elena nodded in agreement. "Yes. It was. But she was scared, Krista, and so confused. A part of her was already gone. She was grasping at what was left."

I sighed and sat back. The hand-drawn maps to the corner store, around our neighborhood, with the descriptions of neighbors' houses, of our own house... I had known on some level that she was struggling, yet I'd wanted her to focus on me for just once in my life. Yet she was lost, had been lost for so long.

"I'm sorry for Mother, I am," I said. "I can't imagine what she was facing. It was all so cruel..."

"But she still had a responsibility to protect you."

"She did," I said to her, staring at the sauna floor. "He came in that night. I was asleep. It took me a minute to realize that he was in my bed, on top of me, before I tried to—" My voice was strangled by old tears.

"I'm sorry, child," Elena murmured.

"He covered my mouth, told me he would kill me and Mother."

"It was all so terrible."

It was why I reacted when Dane pulled me to him… I could see it now.

"You came, Elena. My knight in shining armor." I smiled through my tears. I could still see her small, round silhouette in the doorway, her cry of outrage. Elena hitting him, slapping him, pounding him, driving him out. But not before the damage had been done—not before I had been so torn apart it took decades to even face that night, fully face it.

"I'm sorry, so sorry," Elena was saying. "I knew William was dangerous. Saw him looking at you. I should have told your mother to quit seeing him, demanded she keep him out of your house. But she was a little happier when he was with her, and I just…didn't."

"Yeah, well, hindsight and all that."

Elena moved forward and reached out her small hands. I took them in mine. "You are an adult now, Krista. You can fight off your own predators. But the biggest one you face is inside you. You know that, don't you?"

I nodded, taking one hand away to brush the tears from my face. "Will you pray for me? I don't know if I have any prayers left in me for myself right now."

Elena immediately closed her eyes and lifted her head, as if seeing Jesus above us in the small cedar room. "Father in heaven," she began, "I ask that you bless this child. I ask you to send these dark memories away. That you help her to find forgiveness in her heart toward her mother. For Krista's sake, as well as Charlotte's. Please Lord. We beg for your help. This will take a great deal of doing, we know. But we also know that she wants to be free of this. Show her the way, Lord. Guide her along the path. In Christ's name, amen."

I squeezed her hands and opened my eyes. "Amen."

There had been no miraculous wave of cleansing, no supernatural phenomena, but I felt a little bit better. I had taken the first step on a different path.

"Thanks, Elena," I said. "Now if I'm going to avoid passing out and seeing some of those visions, I'd better get some cool, dry air."

"You have to tell him," Elena said, emerging from the sauna behind me. "You have to tell Dane what happened."

"I know. I'm trying to find the courage. I'm *trying*," I repeated in exasperation when Elena still stared at me.

The next morning I returned to Cimarron. Mother was holding steady, with basically no change in the last seventy-two hours, according to her chart.

My mind was on Dane anyway. I ducked out of her room and waved at the nurse. "Can we take Mother to the Christmas room this afternoon?"

"I don't see why not. Just let me know when you're ready, and we'll help you down there."

"Thanks. Hey, have you seen Dane today?"

She paused for a telltale second. "Think I saw him headin' toward the chapel, but that was 'bout an hour ago."

"I'll start there," I said.

The chapel was to the left of the administration wing. Small and long, it had beautiful, clear glass with a wave to it that made me think of water. There were three chairs on either side with perhaps ten rows total. Once a month a visiting pastor held services here. But it was a tough job, with congregants who were as likely to get up and try to outpreach you as they were to wander out the doors at any time.

Yet the pastors had learned to be accommodating to the peculiarities of Alzheimer's and could often be found searching the halls to serve Communion to any believers who desired it.

Dane was in the front row on the right, his head in his hands. Praying? I moved forward and slid into the first chair on the left, one row back from him.

He angled me a look. "Krista." My name came out in a near whisper. He still stared forward, his eyes on the Mexican-carved wooden cross? The tiny altar table?

"I owe you an apology."

"I think it's I who owe you the apology."

"No—"

A patient wandered in, her hands full of plastic flowers from the arboretum. She walked past us, muttered about vases and water, the indignity of *these cheap flowers,* paced up front for a moment, then left the plastic tulips and daisies on the altar, apparently deciding they didn't need water after all.

Dane crossed the center aisle and sat in front of me, turning on the seat to look into my eyes. "I shouldn't have pushed."

"I was sexually assaulted when I was seventeen," I said. It came out in a rush before I chickened out.

He looked as if I had hit him, dumbfounded for a long moment. Then understanding set his eyes afire. "All this time…"

He didn't finish his sentence. What had he wanted to say? *All this time that's why you've pushed me away. Why we never got back together.*

"It was a man who Mother was seeing. Elena came, but not before…"

Dane grew pale, and he shook his head. It wasn't often that I witnessed Dane McConnell grow speechless. It made me all the more nervous.

"It left me with some issues. Just topped off my barrel with Mother and with men…" I could feel my face growing hot. "I thought it was in the past, something I could forget. But it wasn't. Apparently I still had to get it out in the open." Like a wound out from under a bandage, in the sun, this was.

"I understand, Krista. Yesterday I thought if I just kissed you, you would see how much…" He let out a laugh that emerged as a scoff. "I was a fool. Talk about exactly the wrong thing to do."

"I…I don't want you to give up. On me." My voice went high

and tight. Would I ever quit crying? "I don't want you to give up on us," I said. Tentatively I reached out a hand.

And when he took my hand in his, I felt as though Jesus had his own hand around ours.

We sat and talked for an hour. About what had happened, what might have been. At long last, it seemed everything was out, leaving me feeling raw and exposed and exhausted.

"Let's get some coffee," Dane suggested after a long moment.

I nodded and rose to follow him out of the chapel. But on our way to the dining hall, one of the nurses came running. "Miss Mueller, come now. Your mother isn't well. Dr. Cunningham is with her now."

I felt my brow furrow in concern. I wasn't ready. Not yet.

We ran behind Joan to the end of the main hall, hung a left, and quickly reached Mother's room. Another nurse, one I didn't recognize, was conferring with Annie. Dr. Cunningham was listening to her breathing with a stethoscope.

An oxygen mask was over Mother's mouth and nose, over the tiny tube already in her nostrils, and her eyes were wide open. A year ago they were frequently open, staring and vacant. But recently they had been shut or at half-mast most of the time. To see them this wide, and her looking so fearful as she labored to breathe, made me fearful too. Her heart monitor squawked out a loud warning.

"Can you do something?" I asked.

"Two milligrams of morphine sulfate," Dr. Cunningham said

to Annie in a low tone. A moment later Annie inserted a needle into Mother's IV.

My attention turned toward Mother. I leaned closer to her and stroked her forehead. "Mother, I'm here. I'm here. It's all right. Try to calm down. Try to take slow, shallow breaths." Congestive heart failure was a cruel asphyxiator. It literally drowned a person in fluid, and the pump failed, flooding the lungs, making the patient more and more anxious for oxygen. The harder the effort to obtain it, the worse it got.

The heart monitor let us all know Mother's heart was pausing, as if considering...

Dane came around the bed and slipped an arm around my shoulders, pulling me backward.

"No! Mother, no! Not yet!" I turned to Dr. Cunningham. "Please. Don't let her die. Not yet. There are things... Please."

The monitor let out an alarm as my mother's heart rate flat lined. We all stared at it without speaking.

Suzanne turned back to search my face and then turned back to the bed. She glanced up at Annie, who mouthed "DNR." We had all signed the paperwork. A year ago. I just couldn't explain it. I knew Mother was ready to die. I thought I was ready for it too. But I wasn't. Not now. Not yet.

"Krista—" Dane began.

"I know, Dane. I know."

The heart monitor still blared its alarm.

"Dr. Cunningham!" I yelled. "Please. Can you bring her back? Just once. Can you try?" I was desperate. This was crazy.

She looked as confused as I felt, still taking in Mother's situation. She glanced at me for a half-second. "I can try. Nothing radical, but if she's on the edge, she'll be back."

"Fine, fine," I said, readily appeased. It was in God's hands now. If he was ready for her to come home, I wouldn't stand in the way any longer.

But I wanted her back. It was astonishingly, profoundly clear to me now—I wasn't ready for Mother to die.

I was fifteen before I knew that something was really wrong with my mother. She had become very confused and disoriented at times. Her hand-drawn maps were all around the house and the car now. Maps that showed each of our neighbors' homes with notes about their colors and distinguishing features written in. She seemed all too aware of her own state; I would find her crying about the slightest thing.

She drove a little but mostly insisted on walking. At night she would make me drive her to the bars. As soon as the sun sank in the west, Mother handed me the keys and told me to do my homework when I got home. She never forgot to say that. Then we would head out, ostensibly to let me practice driving, but I was still nine months from getting my license, and I didn't like driving at night any more than she did. Yet I did as she asked. What could I do?

Leaving her on the sidewalk in front of the Silver Spur or Adobe Bar, seeing her disappear through the blackened doorway after telling me to "be a good girl," when I knew she was about to be anything but…I felt somehow dirtied by her actions, by my part in them.

I would drive home, five miles under the speed limit because I thought it made me less conspicuous.

Quiet house. Dark house. Lonely house. Homework done in the stark light of the kitchen table lamp. Idle time on the phone with Blair or Dane. TV dinners. I missed my mother then, sometimes.

The thing was, when she got home, it just seemed all the lonelier.

Chapter Ten

Dane touched my shoulder, and I woke to find him kneeling beside me. It was well past midnight, in those confusing hours of not-quite morning. The question still hung in his eyes. Why had I pushed to bring Mother back? Do-not-resuscitate orders only worked if the survivors weren't in the room demanding that medical personnel save their loved one. I had put the staff in a horrible position by changing my mind at the eleventh hour.

Still, I didn't want to answer Dane's question. I hadn't answered it for myself. I shifted in the deep chair, unfolding my stiff legs and back from their crooked positions, and looked over at Mother, who seemed to be resting more comfortably now. At least her eyes were closed and her breathing was a little easier.

What was going on in her head? Had she glimpsed heaven? Did she wonder why she wasn't there now?

"You know what I wanted for Christmas when I was four?" I said, rubbing my eyes and cheeks. I had gone to sleep reading

Mother's journal entries, remembering Christmases past. In 1970 Mother divorced my absentee father and was attempting to raise me "with some modicum of dignity and hope," as she said. Oma and Opa were already not doing well physically. For the first time, in reading that entry, it hit me that my mother felt desperately alone. That she probably never again felt any connection with an adult other than Elena.

Dane shook his head "What'd you want?"

"For Daddy to come home. I told Santa, my mother, my Opa and Oma, the mailman, anybody who would listen. I figured if I said it enough, told enough people, it would come true."

"Did you get what you wanted?"

"Nah." I hung my head and let out a heavy sigh.

"Sometimes wishes don't come true."

"And sometimes they do." I threw him a sad smile, then nodded over at Mother. "I don't know why."

"Only God knows why. You and he better get it straight soon though, because Suzanne won't keep rushing in to bring Charlotte back again and again. Your mother's been through enough, Krista. Her body is as tired as her mind. It's time to let her go."

I sat back and the cushion let out a long *whoosh* sound. "I know that. You think I don't know that?"

Dane nodded, a fast, shallow wave of his head in quick support. But his eyes remained firm, relentless. "You need to resolve this, Krista. With her." He stared at me for a long moment, then rose and gestured with his hand for me to do the same. Obediently I rose, any pride left within now beaten down.

Working quickly, he pulled the cushions off the chair and then tugged up on the bottom. In amazement I watched as it turned into a makeshift bed. He went to the closet and got out a couple of blankets and a pillow. In another minute the bed was ready for me. "Get some sleep, Krista," he said. He drew me close for a hug, kissed my forehead, and then he was gone. I immediately felt a chill where his body heat had warmed me. What would it be like to hold on to that warmth and never let it go?

I turned to Mother and touched her cool cheek. Her skin felt like wrinkly, soft paper. Was it her warmth I was missing? The child in me wanted her to rise, to invite me into her lap, to hold me as though she never wanted to let *me* go. I laughed at myself. I outweighed her by fifty pounds. But there was no getting around it. That was what I wanted. Longed for.

Too numb to think about anything more, I pulled off my sweater and slipped under the hospital blankets on the foldout bed. Staring at Mother—so frail, so empty, so sick—until my eyelids felt more like ten-pound weights than skin, I finally closed them and slept.

I awakened at seven to a new nurse washing Mother's skin, turning her so she wouldn't get bedsores. "Roll on over here, Miz Charlotte. There ya go." She hummed "Beautiful Savior" under her breath. Bosomy and black, about my age, she looked at me with soft eyes as I roused. "Heard you almost lost your mama last night."

I nodded. I'd felt as though I lost my *mama* before I was two.

The lady in the bed was simply *Mother* as long as I could remember naming her anything at all. "Yeah. I'm Krista. Where's Annie?"

"I'm Rolanda. Seems I was on shift when you weren't about. But I heard you were here. Annie's off this week. On vacation. She came in and said good-bye to Miz Charlotte while you were sleeping. You didn't hear her?"

I shook my head. "Must've been sleeping really deeply."

"M'm-h'm. That's what Annie tol' me."

"You probably heard I played the part of the unreasonable daughter last night too."

"That, too," she agreed without argument, but she looked at me with a sly grin. "Want a cup of coffee?"

"I'd kill for one."

"Thought you might. You go down and get yourself some hot java and breakfast. I'll make sure your mama doesn't die on my shift."

"Thanks," I said, feeling sheepish as I rolled off the bed.

"Losing your mama can make a grown woman crazy," Rolanda said, still working on Charlotte. "Don't question yourself, girl. Just go with your gut. What Doc Cunningham did to bring her back… No ma'am, I've never seen a patient come back like that. You might not be ready to say good-bye, but old Charlotte here wasn't ready either."

I nodded, and my eyes ran over Mother's white skin, taut with bloating liquid. I slipped on my sweater, pulled a brush out of my purse, and ran it through my hair and looked into the mirror. It wasn't so bad. I looked a little better than road kill.

"Never you mind your bed-rumpled looks. Go get that coffee. The world will look a little brighter with a cup in you."

I laughed. Rolanda and I were going to get along just fine. It was a gift, what she had, that ability to make strangers feel like old friends from the get-go. With a wave I left the room and walked to the dining hall.

Dane had designed the dining room with semicognizant patients in mind. There were several family-sized dinner tables with warm chandeliers and inviting, homey wallpaper on the walls. To one side was an old-fashioned counter in vivid red and steel barstools with red leather seats. Behind the counter was a long mirror, reminiscent of old ice cream parlors. There one could get an ice cream sundae or coffee or a soda or a cup of soup. The fast and simple things. Except no one was manning the station right now. I could see the carafe steaming on a warm burner just out of reach.

I looked around, and observing two staff people busy serving two tables of patients, I lifted the folding countertop and went behind to pour myself a cup of coffee.

"Make that two," Dane said from behind me.

My eyes met his in the mirror. "You should be the one back here. We were heading for a cup last night when Mother took her turn."

"Next time I'll pour."

I got out another white cup and saucer from beneath the counter and fixed us each a cup. I braced myself for conversation. But Dane simply picked up his cup, raised it toward me with a smile of thanks, and left.

I leaned on the bar and studied the empty doorway. What was this? No questions? No soul-searching queries? No torturous interrogation as to what I was thinking last night?

I laughed at myself. No. He knew I'd already be running myself through the obstacle course myself. Except I found myself mired in the mud pool, the rope swinging just out of reach.

More coffee. That was what I needed. And a Danish. I raised the glass lid and took a cream cheese Danish out and set it on a plate. Cream cheese Danishes were famous for fixing the worst of problems.

It was only as I was walking back to Mother's room that I saw the date. To keep patients from chronically asking what day it was, what year it was, what time it was, clocks and calendars were literally everywhere. December 21. Tonight was the town dance in the plaza. My mind went to my car's front seat, where the costume Dane had given me still sat, hastily rewrapped in the tissue. What was I going to do?

My first thought was that it was impossible. I couldn't go from my dying mother's bedside to a town dance. My second thought was that that would be exactly where Charlotte would want me to be—dancing. I entered Mother's room just as Rolanda was leaving. "Got that coffee down?" she asked.

"Yes. And you were right. It was just what I needed." I raised a fresh mug toward her. "Brought you this."

"You are a godsend, girlfriend. Thank you."

"I brought it black. I didn't know…"

She smiled at me, and I noticed how her grin lit up her eyes. "Got my Sweet'n Low behind the station counter. Thanks again." She disappeared, leaving my mother and me alone again.

I sank down to the chair, remade now into its original formation, the blankets neatly stacked on the closet shelf, and looked over at Mother. "What should I do? You're not doing well, and obviously I'm having trouble saying good-bye to you. But Dane wants me to come. It's been a long time since I've danced." A dark thought raced through my mind. What if I couldn't remember? What if the steps eluded me and I stumbled and made a fool of myself?

"Maybe I should just stay here, not go to the dance," I mumbled.

"You will go," Elena said, entering the room and placing a fresh bouquet of roses by Mother.

"Those are beautiful, Elena."

"Good. They're for you as much as they're for Charlotte. She can smell them at least." She turned to me. "She'd want you to go."

"I'm not so sure."

"What? She loved to see you dance."

"My mother loved to watch me dance the dances *she* taught me."

"In her own way she loved you, child."

I didn't respond.

"Go, Krista. I will stay here with Charlotte."

I paced my room at Elena's until nine trying to get my courage up, telling myself I'd leave in another fifteen minutes, over and over until it was 9:15, then 9:30. The dance would be in full swing by now. Had Dane given up on my arrival? He had never mentioned it to me today. Never asked if I intended on answering his request for just one dance. Maybe he took my silence as a no.

I closed the bathroom door again to stare at myself in the full-length mirror. The costume Dane had chosen was stunning. I couldn't very well take it off and go to bed. That would be inexpressibly sad, and I'd just have one more thing to talk over with my counselor. No, my counselor would tell me to go, to explore this feeling of desire and curiosity and life and see where it led me. *Choose the new road for once, Krista,* he'd say. *Quit following the old road.* I could hear his voice ringing in my ears. Because now my gut was speaking loud and clear, and it sounded just like him.

"All right. All right, all right, all right!" I said, as if miffed that my heart was telling me what to do. But as I drove toward town, observing the traditional bonfires on private land, the *farolitos*—candles in warmly glowing paper bags along adobe walls—I couldn't keep the smile from my face.

It was so good to be home. So good to be in this land where people came to reinvent themselves, where others stayed to honor their heritage. In this land where the elements were so clear—earth and sky and wind and water, and faith and hope and community—I felt clearer on who I was, who I was born to be. I felt more vivid, more alive, here than anyplace else. I was Krista Mueller. And I was a dancer. Tonight I would dance again as I hadn't in a decade. I would revel in life.

Facing Mother's death had suddenly made it imperative.

So it was that I neared the laughing and clapping and singing people—old Indian couples swaying together, still in love; then young Mexican girls in gay colored costumes, swirling, swirling across the dance floor; then sultry Spanish dancers with their black hair pulled back in severe buns while their eyes spoke of soft passions.

I smiled as one song melted into another, three *flamenco* dancers stomping out the old gypsy dance with gusto now, my eyes searching through the crowd of Taoseños and tourists, sifting through them to find the man I sought. Where was he? I swallowed hard, my throat dry when I thought of him waiting on me and giving up in disgust. But that wasn't Dane's way. He was patient, always patient, waiting for me, watching. He had invited me. Dared me to dance. Dared me to live. Dared me to remember.

He was here. I just hadn't found him yet. On and on I searched, weaving through the laughing, cheering people.

The mariachi band finished the *cuadrilla,* a square-dance song, and began playing the music to a chotís, the ancient two-step I loved.

"Is this the one?" Dane said, speaking lowly in my ear. He had sneaked up on me with the stealth of an Apache hunter. I swallowed the shiver of anticipation, ducked my head, and turned to him with a smile.

He took my hands and spread them out, looking me over from

head to toe, and shaking his head in wonder. I was certain I turned scarlet at his frank approval. "I'm sure you know you're gorgeous," he said, tucking my hand into the crook of his arm. "But in case you don't, be assured you are." His eyes held mine more boldly than they had since high school. Back when he was sure we would be together forever. Before I had beaten such nonsense out of his heart and head.

He led me to the dance floor, and we faced forward, with his arm behind my waist, his fingers gently but firmly on my left hip, his right hand holding my right. We stepped in sync with the other dancers. Some were as old as eighty, dancing as they had for decades, some as young as twelve, clearly uneasy, silently mouthing the count, but wanting to take part. Being a part of the circle, with the ancient music and the scent of burning cedar and piñon pine from the bonfires and the soft, warm light from farolitos all about, brought home to me all that had become clear as I neared the plaza. Life. How long had it been since I had embraced life?

Dane stared at me with each turn. Everything beyond him swirled in a mad profusion of color and smell and movement, yet he and I stayed static, as if held in space. "You look...amazing." *Different,* he wanted to say. I could tell. The song ended, but we just stood there, staring at each other.

"It's me smiling," I said stupidly, as if he couldn't see it himself. But I was saying so much more. "I'm smiling, Dane, and I can't seem to stop." Then the tears came, and they were dripping so fast I had to pull my hand from his to wipe them away.

"Yes, yes, it *is* you smiling," he said. He never thought me foolish. He loved me. He had always loved me.

Another dance began, and he pulled me to the edge of the crowd and then through it. He pulled me through an arched doorway and then another and another until we emerged in a tiny, secluded plaza—someone's private yard—surrounded by the flickering warm lights of farolitos. He pulled me to the corner of two walls and placed me there with such deference that I felt more like a statue of Santa María than myself. But I remained still, obedient to follow, to trust for once, fascinated by his actions, curious beyond all measure to see what would come next.

"I came to dance," I tried, feeling the tiniest urge to go back to my old defenses. I sniffed, the tears finally slowing but still falling.

"And we danced our dance," he said. "It was all I hoped it would be, Krista. My Kristabelle." His voice ached with need. "Now, shh."

He took the tip of my shawl and gently wiped the tears from my eyes. He settled it about me again and then slowly ran his fingers down my arms until he could take my hands in his.

His eyes, filled with concern, lifted to meet mine as he held one of my hands before me. "You're trembling."

I could say nothing in response, only wait for him to know, to understand somehow.

"Are you frightened?"

"Yes," I whispered. "But…I want you to kiss me."

Then he took my face in his big, strong hands and, as I had

done on the bridge, slowly, reverently kissed one cheek, unhurriedly moved to kiss the other, bent my head to kiss my forehead, and then stared into my eyes until the tears came running again. I was trembling from head to toe.

A blackness was at the edge of my vision, a dark wall threatening to reach up and swallow my happiness—an abyss that made me want to run before it was too late, before...

I swallowed my fear, forced myself to stay in the moment to swallow life and light and love...to let Dane kiss me as I'd wanted to let him when I was a teen. It was then that his pager started singing.

We laughed, both acknowledging the unfortunate interruption, but without taking his eyes off me, Dane flipped it off with one hand. He brought his hand back to my face then, and I welcomed its returning warmth, the way he touched me with such deference, appreciation, peace. Nudging closer, he stared into my eyes as our bodies touched. Gently, sweetly, he bent to kiss me then.

And I let him.

More than that, I kissed him back.

It was a sorry day that I discovered my mother in her old dance studio. As a junior in high school, involved in advanced placement classes and drama and dance, I didn't arrive until well after dark. It worked well, my schedule. I didn't have to deal with my mother; she didn't have to deal with me. If we had felt separated before, the chasm between us now was death-defying.

Without me to drive her, she had quit barhopping. For a couple of years, the men seemed to find her, but even that had stopped, much to my relief. She returned to her pattern of drawn drapes, long showers, and hours in front of the television. Most Sundays I could convince her to dress and go to church, but she hung back, anxious to go home afterward, as if afraid that if we didn't go home right away, we might never get home again.

I was pretty sure by then that she was losing it. I didn't have the name, the diagnosis, but I knew that what was happening to Mother was beyond her control.

So when I came home that night, ready to make us supper, and discovered her bed empty, I grew concerned.

I finally found her outside, in the old studio where she had taught *me the ways of the old ones, the ancient steps. She was a silhouette in the moonlight streaming in the windows, wandering, wandering.*

"Mother?" *I asked. I rubbed my arms. It was freezing. She had to be cold. I could see her in the dim light, dressed in the traditional garb.*

"I've forgotten," *she said.*

I thought about turning on the lights but knew the sudden brightness would confuse her further. "What? What have you forgotten, Mother?"

"The steps. To the cuna. Can you imagine?"

She sounded so forlorn, so lost, that I faltered. The cuna was the first dance she had ever taught me. I didn't know what to say.

"Krista, how could I have forgotten the steps to the cuna?"

Chapter Eleven

I left Dane in that picturesque little patio and walked directly to my car. He let me go, silently watching as I left, knowing it was for the best. If I felt trapped, I would run. And neither of us wanted me to run right now. This was it. We were going to either fish or cut bait. I didn't know about Dane, but I felt as if I had a champion bass on the end of a very fragile, frayed line.

I went back to Cimarron and ducked my head in embarrassed pleasure when the aides and nurses smiled their appreciation of my festive dress. I stood in Mother's room until midnight, listening to one Spanish CD after another, patting out the beat on her arm so she might take part in the dance in some small way. Outside it had begun to snow again. I talked to her about the colors, the light, the music. Of how good it felt to be a part of the plaza and community again. How good it felt to dance. That was when it occurred to me.

I studied Mother as the dim light from the hallway fell on her.

She had had a good day in comparison with yesterday. Her breathing was a little easier. There was only one tube connecting the oxygen to her nose. Carefully I selected a song she had loved as a young woman, "Estrellita," and then pressed Play. The dreamy, soothing music from flute and guitar filled the room. Moving to Mother, I slid my arms under her knees and shoulders and lifted her.

She was surprisingly light. Conscious of the tube that bound her to within a few feet of the bed, I made up a simple, swaying, two-step pattern to the beat. I wanted her to feel what I had experienced again this night, the feeling of music entering the ears and emerging in the flow of movement, of life. Back and forth we moved, and I was amazed at the sweetness of it. Mother had taught me to dance. Here I was, leading her in the last dance she would ever take. The Christmas music had moved through the tangles of neurons that strangled her brain; I hoped the Spanish notes would do so too.

"Do you remember, Mother?" I whispered. "Do you remember feeling young and beautiful and alive? Do you remember how you taught Dane and me to let the music move through us?"

I was tiring, and the song was coming to an end. Gently I set her down on the bed and covered her with the blanket. That was when I felt her cold fingers on my arm. And the smallest movement. Was that an attempt at a squeeze?

My eyes flew to her face. A single tear ran down her weathered cheek like a shining rivulet across the desert floor in the moonlight. A lump grew in my throat. I sank to my knees beside

Mother's bed and whispered, "Oh, Mother, you're welcome. I...I liked it too."

"What you think this is, girl? A B&B?" Rolanda asked the next morning, waking me as she made her rounds.

I sat up from my makeshift bed, smiling as I rubbed my eyes. "Oh hi, Rolanda. It would be a sad B&B if that's what I was looking for."

"You got that right."

"Rolanda, last night...last night I took up Mother in my arms and danced with her. This might sound crazy—"

"Not much is called crazy around here," she said with a smile.

"I think...I think she might've responded. I think she tried to squeeze my arm."

Rolanda smiled over at me as she rolled Mother over to shift her position. "I'm not surprised. That was very thoughtful. She was a dancer once, I take it."

"Yes. A very good one. She taught me. And Dane." In my enthusiasm it just slipped out.

"*Our* Dane McConnell? He dances too, does he? There isn't a thing that man can't seem to do."

I nodded in silent agreement.

"Oh, I recognize that look." Her eyes shifted to my dance costume thrown over another chair. "You didn't happen to dance with someone besides your dear old mama last night, did you?"

"Just one dance," I said with a shy grin.

"M'm-h'm," she said smugly. She folded her arms over her ample chest. "Just one thing I want you to do. Don't you dare break that dear man's heart. It's high time he found himself a woman. He don't have time for no tomfoolery."

"No tomfoolery. Got it."

"Don't you make fun of me. We just met."

"Oh, I see. You can tease me, but I can't give it back to you."

"That's right," she said, folding a towel and setting it by the sink. "Now you got the way of things." She leaned down toward Mother. "You did good, Charlotte, teaching these children to dance." With a pat to Charlotte's arm and another smile for me, she left the room.

I pulled my hair back into a ponytail and brushed my teeth at the sink. I looked all right this morning. There was something about my eyes…

"You're up bright and early," he said from the door.

I looked up quickly. "Dane. Good morning."

"I came around and watched you sleeping," he said, sheepishly shoving his hands in his pockets.

"Oh no. Was I drooling?"

"Only a little. I put a bucket under you and left you to your slumber."

"Thanks," I said, managing to smile at his teasing.

He stayed in the doorway, as if still afraid of spooking me, sending me running. He shoved his hands into his pockets. "Actually, you never looked lovelier. You were…peaceful."

I nodded. I felt peaceful. Dancing with Mother had broken a

barrier within me, made me feel somehow a little more whole. Not to mention how dancing with Dane had made me feel or his kiss...

"Want to grab some lunch today?" Dane asked.

"Sure. 'Bout 11:30?"

"Sounds good. I'll be back for you then."

I turned and made up my bed into its original chair position, and opened the book of Christmas carols. Mother's next entry read:

Christmas 1975

It is beyond me how Marc can ignore our beautiful Krista. She yearns for her daddy, asks why he doesn't come to America more. I have explained his absences away by telling her that he is a French citizen, an incredibly busy foreign correspondent who travels to everywhere but New Mexico. Still, I can tell the explanation is wearing thin. There is something in her eyes that tells me she takes his absence personally, thinking that if she were better behaved or prettier or nicer he would come home to stay. I don't know how to tell her that he's never coming home. But I must. Last year I divorced him. And with the signed papers, I knew we would never see him again.

I'm fifty-three years old now and feel like I am just getting my life together. Some day maybe Krista will understand that she can never find the acceptance she yearns for in a man's eyes. The only man who will ever love her without condition is Jesus. It has taken me decades to learn that validation, respect, and true devotion can be echoed in man but only seen without error in God. I pray that she comes to this understanding sooner than I did.

Krista, my beloved, if you ever do read this note, know that you are all a mother could ask for, that you are beautiful and kind and smart. I find it hard to make these words come from my mouth. I am imperfect in this way, among many other imperfections. My prayer is that one day you might understand.

They were lovely words, longed-for words, but they made no sense. I let the book fall to my lap. Mother had felt love for me, devotion, once. She sounded defensive for me, angry at my father for never coming to the States to see me. I didn't have the father I deserved. No one to call me "Daddy's little girl." He had been a lout. Mother had made a poor choice in marrying him, but could I hold her poor choice over her head forever? No.

"Oh, God," I whispered, looking up at the ceiling, "I think I've been mad at Mother all these years for not giving me a dad, when it was really never her choice. Please forgive me. Please help me see things better. In your light, Lord. Amen."

I looked over at Mother and took her hand in mine. Her eyes were shut, her breathing at odd intervals. "All these years, Mother, I wanted an apology for that, too... I'm sorry."

I sat back, letting her limp hand drop from mine back to the bed. And studying her. There were many things that still didn't make sense to me. Her obvious deepening faith contrasted starkly with what I knew came later in life. My mother had been loose, promiscuous, by the time I was fourteen or fifteen. A parade of boyfriends cascaded through my head. They had been ugly years, those years when Charlotte was losing her memory but not her looks.

I opened the book of carols again and studied the song she had chosen to write under "I Heard the Bells on Christmas Day." My eyes kept running over the same verse: *"God is not dead, nor doth He sleep. The wrong shall fail, the right prevail. With peace on earth, good will to men."*

"No, Mom," I said, letting the more intimate name roll off my tongue and hang in the air between us. "God isn't dead. He isn't asleep. I get it. I get what you were trying to tell me. You figured out you could quit trying to bring justice to the world, right? That God would see to it, and you could simply look for peace."

She didn't beg my forgiveness, couldn't look over at me and nod, couldn't smile at me with love in her eyes, as I longed for, but my words sounded right to me. True. Good. It was a start anyway. "That you, Lord?" I whispered. I hadn't felt such a wave of peace, such hope, for years. The air felt supercharged with energy, and I sat back to bask in it as if it were a down comforter. And then I smiled.

"So you slept here," said Elena, walking in the door.

"Oh. Yes. I'm sorry I didn't call—"

"No worries. But I had hoped you were dancing all night, not just sitting by my old friend's bedside."

"Oh, I danced all right."

Her dark eyes met mine, and we smiled.

I was twenty years old, and instead of leaving home, chasing my own dreams, I found myself stuck in our tiny house, driving the miles to and from a college in Santa Fe—St. John's College—so I could help care for my ailing mother. I arrived home to find Elena in our kitchen, stirring a pot of soup. She was humming a haunting Christmas carol, and the words ran through my head as I kissed her on the cheek and went to my room to dump my stuff. "O come, O come, Emmanuel, and ransom captive Israel that mourns in lonely exile here until the Son of God appear. Rejoice! Rejoice! Emmanuel shall come to thee, O Israel."

Mother was in the living room, rocking in her La-Z-Boy, rocking fast and hard. I didn't know what I would do without Elena. Mother took constant care now, and it was exhausting. Constant questions, constant rambling, constant roaming.

What scared me most was her health. She was all of sixty-three years old. Her mind was diminishing, the diagnosis now a firm Alzheimer's, but outwardly she seemed as strong as an ox. No release in an early death for us, I thought angrily. No, it was just one more way Mother was going to get me. Living on, making life miserable. Making me work for everything I had, including a moment's peace.

Elena hummed louder, as if reading my thoughts, wanting to remind me of my own ransom, my own measure of grace. I ignored her.

"Krista?" Mother called. "Krista, that you? Time for dinner! I got some TV dinners. Have you done your homework? Krista? Krista? Krista?"

I stood there in the doorway, arms crossed, watching my mother. She never turned around, just sat there, shouting, shouting from another time. When I didn't answer, she quieted. On and on she rocked.

Chapter Twelve

December 23

My eyes shifted from the words on the page of Mother's journal to Mother herself. How many years had she longed for connection, relationship, association? Trapped in the mire of familial loyalty and pity and desire for a mom I would never have, I had simply become more furious with each passing day. Alzheimer's slow rot and my arrested growth entwined in a frenetic, caustic life. Simply put, Mother and I had been miserable.

Over and over I would endeavor to begin anew. If Reagan and Gorbachev could do it, I'd reasoned, so could we. We'd have a decent day or two, and then something would set one of us off.

Dane had left for school two years earlier, probably relieved to be free of our declining friendship and evaporated romance. My life was now all about me and Dear Old Mom. I studied at St. John's College three days a week, taking a full load, alternating care with Elena. But trying to study at home was difficult: Mother wanted to know what I was reading, then asked me again and again. I simmered under my carefully laid facade, ready to blow like the Colombian volcano that took out twenty-five thousand lives in one fell swoop that year.

And while I fought the suffocation, desperate to break free, Mother continued to throw out her web. The truth was she was trying to reach out to me, but the closer she got, the more I wanted to be anywhere but there. It was as if we had missed the bridge that would connect us and were walking along the ravine, sometimes drawing near, sometimes yelling across a gaping distance. But when we got to those drawing-near places, I knew it wouldn't work; it had never worked. And Mother's obvious desperation to cross made me suddenly eager to get farther away.

Her note dated "1885"—really 1985—only made me feel more lousy about it now. I had failed her. Again and again I failed her, just as she failed me.

This was how she saw things at the time:

I am sixty-some years old and find myself terribly lonely. Krista lives with me, but in her heart, she is far away. I want what other mothers have with their daughters. But we can't seem to find our connection or peace between us. I irritate her, I think, with my forgetting ways. And the more this quiet panic sets in, the more I want her to hold my hand, hold me and tell me it will be all right. But it was never that way between us. I can't remember if I ever held her as a child, ever told her it would be all right. I can't remember if that's because it never happened or just that I can't remember. There's so much I can't remember. I have forgotten so much. It makes me crazy, this forgetting. It's just beyond my reach, still present in my head, but I can't get to it. I want to reach up and cut it out, hold it, show it to the world. Show them that I am not stupid. That I am still me. But I'm not me. Not at all. Day by day I lose another little piece of myself and a piece of what might have been with my daughter.

My eyes misted with that last sentence. So I hadn't been alone in my desire for something more, something better between us. She had wanted me too. The whole thing was like a Greek tragedy really, with each of us trying to come together but hubris and circumstances prying us apart. How I fantasized about Mother coming after me, dropping to her knees in weepy apologies, swearing her love, begging forgiveness! My nose grew hot, as it did when I was about to cry. What a fool I had been. What a sorry, pathetic, miserable disciple of Christ.

"Lord God, I'm sorry," I whispered, looking to the ceiling.

I glanced over at Mother, my eyes swimming in tears. She was so frail, laboring on. She and I had been like captives, hauled in different directions. We had merely passed each other, never met on common ground. She had understood the power of Christ's ransom, yet I'd been too busy to notice. She had wanted me once. Maybe she had always wanted me. I just hadn't wanted her at the same time. The tears streamed down my cheeks, and I sniffed, reaching for a tissue.

Mother's lifting and falling chest drew my attention. How fine it would be for her when she could stop struggling, could take her first deep, clear breath in heaven. I had to let her go. But first I had to do something. I rose, closed the room door, and went to Mother, knowing I only had a few minutes before a caregiver would come in. Her hand was cold and thin, the veins blue beneath wide sun spots.

"You always did like too much sun, Mother," I said, holding her hand in my left hand while tentatively stroking her face, her hair. "You'd have a fit with the amount of sunscreen they expect us to wear today."

I watched the IV drip fluid into the tube that led into the back of her hand, shifted my vision to the machine that rose and dropped with each breath of air, then looked back to her face. Her eyes were open, wide and staring, for the first time in days. I took a half-step backward, shocked, surprised to see her eyes—"ocean blue" as Marc called them in his love letters—trained on me.

"M-Mother?" I asked. "Mother? It's me, Krista. I'm here, Mother. I'm here." It hadn't taken much. This one last smidgen of connection had me weeping.

We stayed in that position for maybe five minutes, me crying my head off, Mother staring vacantly somewhere in my direction. I didn't know if she knew me, didn't know if she remembered having a child at all.

Finally I managed to speak. "Remember that Christmas when I was five and Oma and Opa had us over for Christmas supper? We had roast beef and creamed potatoes, and the house smelled of baking bread and pine tree and Opa's pipe. There were presents under the tree and German glass ornaments on it."

I focused on Mother again. Her eyes were on the far wall. But they were filled with tears too. I reached for another tissue and wiped her dripping nose, then the tears as they fell. "We laughed then, Mother. You and Oma and Opa and I. I don't remember why, but I remember we *laughed*."

I cried harder then. I hadn't remembered ever laughing with Mother until now. The memory sewed together a tiny rift in my heart. "Oma would pester Opa to put out his pipe, but I loved the smell so much I'd ask him to blow smoke in my face. Remember? Oma made me a red sweater, and Opa made me a dollhouse. It was a good Christmas. The best. Do you remember, Mother?

"Mother, I want you to know that I'm going to work at remembering those happy memories. Times when you and I were closer. I'm going to remember that you tried and you wanted me and that you loved me. I'm sorry, Mother. I'm sorry we could never get it together. I'm sorry."

Mother still cried, but her eyes did not shift to me. Slowly I lowered my head to her chest and continued to apologize and cry, and the weird thing was, the more I apologized, the more I felt empathy and forgiveness for her.

Grace is like that. The more you give, the more you gain.

It was Dane who finally entered the room with a gentle knock and found me sniffling and snuffling.

"I'm sorry," he said. "Want me to come back?"

"No," I said, shaking my head. "Come here." I waved him forward and pulled him into my arms. "I need someone to hold me, Dane. Mother can't hold me. I think she would if she could. But she can't."

Tentatively he did as I asked, gradually relaxing and cradling my head with his hand, giving me tiny, reassuring kisses until I stopped crying. When I was still, he said, "So you did it finally, huh?" He looked over at Charlotte and gently stroked her hand while still holding me.

"Yeah, I did."

"How do you feel?"

I paused a moment, then smiled. "Better."

"That's good."

"Yeah, it is. You know what would make it even better?"

"What?"

"Kissing you."

He pulled back a little to look in my eyes. "Are you offering that because you are really ready for it or because you're feeling low?"

"Maybe a little of both."

He thought on that for a long moment, and in that pause I felt the desire that warmed me from my knees to my scalp. I wanted Dane McConnell to kiss me. I wanted to kiss him. There wasn't an ounce of fear in me. He was waiting for me to make the first move, intent on making sure he didn't scare me again.

So when we kissed, it started gentle and sweet, then became more heated, searching, longing. When we parted, both of us were teary even as we smiled. He stared at me, as if in wonder, touching my hair, my cheek, my shoulder as if I were an apparition, liable to disappear at any second.

I smiled. "I'm here, Dane. I'm really here."

"Yes. Yes, you are, Kristabelle."

And when I sank into his arms again, soaking in the love of his embrace like a sponge in warm water, I knew that a part of me I thought would never be retrieved was quietly molding itself back into my heart.

Dr. Cunningham entered after a brief knock. A heated wave of red climbed up her neck to her cheeks when she saw us. Dane and I parted guiltily, as if we were a pair of illicit lovers. She feigned a smile and immediately turned to Charlotte's chart. I felt badly for her, as if I had snatched up the last croissant at Starbucks right in front of a starving woman. But it was meant to be. Dane and I were meant to be. I'd been too stubborn to see it.

She turned to me, her eyes dull, and I felt another arrow of guilt.

"Krista," she said, looking to Mother's chart again. She was all caring doctor again, any trace of interest in Dane now firmly under control. "Your mother is on the maximum dosage of dobutamine. It sounds to me like her left lung is pretty full of fluid. Her right is working at about half capacity, but at this rate the meds won't be able to make a difference for much longer." She reached out, touched my arm, and looked into my eyes again.

"Oh," was all I could manage. "Is there anything more you can do to make her more comfortable?"

"We've done all we can," she said, telling me what I already assumed.

I nodded. "Thank you, Doctor."

She glanced at Dane once and then paused in the doorway, looking back at me. "I'm sorry, but I need to ask about your Mother's DNR form and your signature—"

I shook my head. "I won't interfere again."

She dropped her chin and then left the room, and we three— Mother, Dane, and I—remained in still silence for several minutes. To me the quiet rang with the death knell of an old church bell. There was little time left. My head raced with scenes of Mexican death parades, of grotesque masks and raised coffins. Lenten symbols to bring home the power of resurrection.

Mother was dying, and this time I would not insist they try to bring her back.

Dane and I wheeled Mother into the Christmas room. The next day would be Christmas Eve, my last Christmas with Mother. So much time wasted.

Dane wrapped an arm around my shoulders and squeezed. "Gotta take what you can get, girl."

"I know. It's just hard. Just when I figure it out, she's leaving me again."

"A lot of her is gone already, Krista. She tried to make her way to the other side last week. Take it as a gift."

"I know," I said again. It still didn't make this parting any easier.

Dane walked to the corner and brought back his guitar, then began playing Christmas carol after Christmas carol. When a few more residents entered the room, he sang the words, and most of them joined in. But not Mother.

Dane could see me watching her, wondering if she would sing. "She liked this one a few weeks ago," he said. But "Jingle Bells" failed to move her to speech.

"Give me one more try," he said. Finding the correct position for his fingers, he began to sing, "O come, O come, Emmanuel, and ransom captive Israel." Wally came right up to Dane then and put an arm around his shoulders as he sang a slightly off-key harmony. "That mourns in lonely exile here until the Son of God appear."

"Rejoice! Rejoice! Emmanuel shall come to thee, O Israel," I joined in, smiling. It was then that I glanced at Mother again. I gasped.

I hadn't heard a word from her in over two years. But she was singing now, in a labored whisper, her eyes open and faraway, as if with Oma and Opa as a child. And her voice was clear and high. "O come, Thou Rod of Jesse, free Thine own from Satan's tyranny. From depths of hell Thy people save, and give them vict'ry o'er the grave."

The words made me cry all the harder. I tried to join in the chorus but could only weep. Was there no end to my tears? It was no use; with every phrase I only wept more. It was as if God had chosen this moment to speak to me, to show me the way to the dawn of my new life.

Dane smiled at me encouragingly. "O come, Thou Dayspring, come and cheer our spirits by Thine advent here; disperse the gloomy clouds of night; death's dark shadows put to flight."

I whispered the final chorus with the rest of them. "Rejoice! Rejoice! Emmanuel shall come to thee, O Israel!" Wally wandered away to finger the chili pepper lights on the tree, mumbling to himself.

Dane set down his guitar and came over to hug me again, smiling down at me and Mother as I bent to kiss her. Her eyes were closed now, her breathing pitiful in its labor. But this final Christmas present was the best one I could have received.

I wrapped an arm around Dane's waist. "Maybe," I said, clearing my throat, "this is what she wanted to say to me. To show me the Christmas room, remind me of what we did have in common all this time."

Dane nodded.

"In here it's Christmas every morning," I said. "And, Dane, what a gift that is, to all of us." I smiled up at him. "If I could just remember Christmas every day of the week, it would change my whole mind-set. Jesus is here. He is present. He is alive. And he came for me." My voice broke. I shook my head in embarrassment over my nonstop tears. But this was important, so important...

"Go on, Krista."

"And he came for me," I forced myself to finish, "just as he came for my mother."

Dane nodded again. He understood.

And at last I did too.

There was a year after Alzheimer's began its ravage that I remember Mother as more coherent, and I was feeling more generous in spirit. We walked, hand in hand, from the car through the snow to Doña Elena's doorway and were welcomed in by the boisterous people inside. I remember it as a year in which we ate with Elena's family at her big table, ate until we were stuffed. Tamales and sopa tortilla and dessert after dessert. I remember large voices and larger gesticulations and laughter. Later, as her grandchildren slumbered, I drove Elena and Mother to church for the candlelight service. I remember that it was late, very late, but it didn't matter because it was Christmas Eve. There was something about the black Christmas sky, alight with desert constellations, that made me wonder if I might see the Bethlehem star. Moving about at such an hour on a wintry night made me feel as if I were in on the great secret, a welcome guest at the most special party in the world.

I remember icons and a towering reredos depicting biblical events, priests chanting mysterious songs. I remember darkness and one lone candle on the altar, shining as bright as a star. I remember a high, clear voice singing a cappella so beautifully that I longed to join in. I remember light from that candle, taken and spread, until the whole sanctuary was alive in the soft glow of candlelight, happy faces in the halo of each one.

I remember.

Chapter Thirteen

December 24

I was able to read Mother's next note—on a card stuck in the book of carols—with a modicum of dignity. It seemed that the days before had dried up my sorrowful cisterns, and in their place, I felt a growing, quiet sense of peace and a sweet yet melancholy acceptance of things as they were.

I had napped by Mother's side through the night, awakening each time I heard a strange sound, sure that each arduous breath would be her last. But still she went on. Mother was always stubborn. It figured she would outlive Suzanne's prediction.

I had dreamed that Elena was showing me how to weave and that Mother was watching us, then holding the shuttle with me, then eventually becoming the weaving itself. I stood back with my arm around Elena and looked her over, her head at the far end, smiling at us, and I said, "Look, Elena! Isn't she beautiful!"

Bleary-eyed, I focused on Suzanne's small grin and cock of the head as she walked into the room. "Can't always predict these things, I guess. Your mother's a strong woman."

"Yes, yes she is," I said, sitting upright. "Listen, Suzanne," I started, eager to clear the air between us. But as she turned around expectantly, my memorized, eloquent speech left me. "I wanted to tell you that I'm sorry. A-about Dane. I hadn't expected… I mean I didn't intend… It just… Oh, brother, I'm not saying this well at all; it kind of just happened. Again. We seem to always get together—but I didn't mean—"

She held up her hand to stop me, and I shushed, half grateful, half embarrassed. Then she gave me another small smile. "Can't always predict these things, I guess," she repeated.

"No. You can't," I said, slowly, wistfully.

"Merry Christmas, Krista."

"Merry Christmas."

She left then, all elegant long legs beneath a crisp white coat. It mystified me why Dane hadn't gotten down on bent knee to propose to the nice woman a year ago. But I was glad he hadn't. I smiled to myself, giddy inside at the idea that Dane and I were back together. After all this time. "Oh, Mother," I said, leaning forward to take her hand, "I think you always wanted me to be with Dane. Maybe that's why I resisted."

I sat back, getting lost in visions of the past, hopes for the future. "I'm in love with him, Mom." I tried out the word, feeling it leave my mouth like a foreign object. "I'm in love with him, Mom," I said, wanting to hear it aloud again—both the loving thing and this new name for my mother. It felt kinder, more intimate. Okay to use now.

"That's good to hear," Dane said from the door. Startled, I did a double take. "Since I am certainly in love with you."

I stared at him. We were saying it. The love word. To each other. Out loud. I felt more like a blushing teenage girl than a woman of thirty-something.

"I did hear you right?" he asked, casually coming closer. His eyes narrowed. "You were speaking of me, right? Not some other guy?" He reached down, and I took his hands, rising to stand in front of him.

"Nope. That would be you I was yammering about to Mother—Mom."

"Mom, is it?"

"Trying it out. What do you think?"

"I like it," he said, wrapping me in his arms. He kissed me on the temple and then pulled back to look me over. "Sleep well?"

"Can't say 'like a log.' More like a splinter. This place is noisy, and Mother… I kept thinking that every odd breath might be her last."

He nodded. "Want me to help keep watch tonight? We could trade off sleep."

"Makes for a bleary-eyed Christmas."

"Well, I've managed to get the next few days off to spend with my love."

"Ah? Know the right people, eh?"

"A few."

I smiled back into his eyes. "Thanks, Dane. It will help to have you with me."

"Why don't you go to Elena's now? Grab a couple hours' sleep, a shower?"

My eyes moved to Mother. "What if?"

He pulled his head to one side. "You've said the important stuff already, right?"

"Yeah, but I want to be with her, make sure she's with someone when she dies."

"I'm somebody."

"Okay. I'll be back soon." I gathered up my purse and coat, suddenly longing for a shower and a little more rest. I kissed Dane as I passed him, then paused at the door. I wanted him to promise me he wouldn't let her die on his watch. That he'd call me if anything changed. That nothing would change. But I knew that he could only do his best, that the situation was out of his hands. What he said was true—the important things had been said.

Still, to be sure, I crossed the room and leaned over Mother. "I love you, Mom." I kissed her softly on the forehead, cast Dane one last smile, and then left the room.

Elena was busy making flour tortillas when I walked in the door. There was little I liked better than a freshly cooked flour tortilla. They had a hint of crispness from the griddle, but the insides were soft and chewy. Creamy butter melted over the surface. I inhaled three before properly addressing Elena.

"Feliz Navidad," I said, rounding the counter at last to kiss her on a round cheek.

"Feliz Navidad," she returned, intent on her work. "I assume you would have called me… Your mother, she's still laboring on?"

"Yes. The doctor thought she'd die anytime last night. She was surprised to see her still at it this morning."

Elena smiled as she rolled a ball of dough in her hands, then patted it into a disk. Her movements were those of a woman who had done this a thousand times before. "She doesn't know your mother then. Didn't know what she was like once."

"No." I sat back at the counter. "I'm beginning to wonder if I ever knew my mother. What she was really like. I've asked you before, Elena. May I ask it again?"

"What?"

"Why did you like Charlotte?" I said it more out of curiosity than any antagonism.

Elena threw the tortilla on the griddle, turned a second, and then picked up another ball of dough. As she rolled and patted, she spoke. "Your mother was a dreamer. She always thought she could do anything…at least when depression didn't rule her. She was strong. She came through a great deal of pain and heartache. A survivor."

My eyes searched the blue Mediterranean tiles of Elena's counter. The same blue of Mother's eyes. My eyes. For the first time it hit me that Elena had lost her husband to cancer about the same time that Mother had divorced Marcellin.

"Losing your husbands," I said, "at about the same time. Did that bring you together?"

"Yes, yes," she said, throwing, turning, rolling another tortilla. "Grief bonds people. You don't know the depths you can sink to until you lose a loved one. And to share that with another…" She stopped rolling for a moment, her eyes lost in another year. "Your mother brought me comfort."

"My mother? To you?"

"Yes," Elena said, going about her work again. "Do not be so surprised. She was capable of giving."

"Just not to me."

"She gave you a home and food and clothing. She taught you to dance. She tried to love you. She did, in her own way. It just never came easy."

"I know."

Her lips thinned and she scowled at me. "I thought you were coming closer, that you might have forgiven her by now."

"I did. Really. I guess…I guess I'm just a little jealous of the relationship you shared with her. Since Mother and I could never connect, I made myself feel better by thinking she never truly loved anyone."

"Very few. She let very few into her heart. But she had been so devastated, Krista. And when she did love, she loved fiercely. She loved you fiercely, even if you never felt it."

"How do you know that?"

"She told me. I could see it in her eyes, in the way she followed your every move and mourned when you were apart."

I gave her a shallow nod of assent. "I found this in the Christmas carol book." I leaned down and pulled an old, yellowed card from my purse and handed it to her. I had read it earlier that day. Elena read it silently.

Calendar says its December 1990, but that cant be write. Somebodys played a trick on me. Gordon could be home any day from the Air Core. FDR and Churchill are making plans with Stalin. Surely, my Gordon will come home now. But Im not sure he can find me. Im locked up with a bunch of loonies like me, and I cant even find my Krista. She left, Krista left, and its Christms, but I haven't seen her. Or maybe shes lost. what if Im supposed to look for her and havent I haven't even gotten out to get a present for her. I wonder if that girl in the hall would take me shopping. I wonder if that girl can tell me where Krista went. She belongs with me. where are you, Krista. where are you.

She handed the card back to me across the bar. "You see?" she said.

"I see. I just wish…" I sighed and shrugged my shoulders. "Can't always get what you wish for, huh?"

"Not always," she returned. "But I'm betting you're also wishing for some rest and a shower."

"Indeed."

"Go. Off with you. I have plans for tonight and will need your help."

"Oh. I told Dane I'd only be gone a short time."

"Yes, yes. Go take your nap and shower, and then I'll tell you the rest before you leave."

Obediently I slid off the stool and padded to the hallway that led to my room. "Thank you, Elena."

"For what? A bit of flour and lard?"

"For everything."

She paused from her work and stared over at me. "Mi hermanita, you don't have to thank me. I've always loved you. You will always have my love, even after your mother goes to be with Jesus."

The nap and shower at Elena's had done a world of good for me. It turned out that all Elena wanted from me was a promise that we would be in Mother's room from six to seven o'clock. Since I knew Dane favored the eleven o'clock candlelight service at church—he had always favored it as a kid anyway—I guessed it would be all right to commit that time. Elena wouldn't tell me why. Just said to be ready and waiting. "Like you would be for the Baby Jesus," she said with a wink.

Mother strained on and on, pausing after exhaling, often for frightful seconds at a time. Just when I thought she couldn't possibly take another breath through the bog that suffocated her, she did so. It was a terrible way to die, this congestive heart failure. I felt guilty for making her live through another week. When I said as much to Dane, he said, "Krista, if it had been the right time for her to die, they wouldn't have been able to bring her back. You two had some unfinished business. I believe that she came back to see it through. As best she could."

"Thanks," I whispered.

At precisely six o'clock, movement outside Mother's window drew my attention. When someone knocked, my eyes focused on a tiny child in a mother's arms. Gradually I recognized the people—all of Elena's family—and when I heard the hum of the pitch pipe, I knew what they were here to do.

Dane smiled and bent over the chair to roll open a long-closed window. Fresh, cold, dry air filtered in, smelling of the desert in hibernation and snow.

"O holy night! The stars are brightly shining," began Elena's granddaughter, Cora, in a high, clear voice. "It is the night of the dear Savior's birth," joined in the girl's father in a fine baritone. On and on they went, each taking a portion of verse, joining together in the triumphant chorus. Vaguely I remembered singing with Oma and Opa at Christmastime, but I'd never been part of a singing family like this one. I knew they would carol tonight and join around the guitar and violin tomorrow for an hour or more of singing—the traditional Anglo carols, the ancient Mexican and Spanish *canciones,* the hymns that always made me cry.

They looked so peaceful, so whole there, all together. Contentment floated around each of them, gradually enveloping us all as we stood listening. God lived with this family; everyone could sense it.

When they finished, I clapped, and Dane joined in. I leaned toward the window. "Thank you, Elena and all you Rodriguezes. That was truly beautiful." I pulled my hand to my heart. "I'll never forget it. Never."

Elena brought her mitten to her lips and sent me a kiss. Then she bent and handed a basket to one of Robbie's boys, a ten-year-old named Armando as strapping as his father had been at that age. He headed off into the darkness. "Meet him at the western entrance, would you, Dane?" Elena asked.

"Sure. Merry Christmas, Elena. Would you all like to come in? Serenade all the folks at Cimarron?"

They looked at each other and, in agreement, moved off to enter the care center. Dane would put them all on stage together, I was sure, and gather the residents to listen. It was almost as exciting as if the von Trapp family were coming to our local little theater. I sat down heavily in the chair. I was sure Elena would pardon my absence. I really did not care to be anywhere but with Mother—Mom—right now. I left her earlier. I had left her so often in these last days, these last years. Now I didn't want to be anywhere else.

Her note haunted me. I had checked her into that first care facility in 1990 and taken off for Colorado to attend graduate school. No wonder she was concerned I had gotten lost. After twenty-five years you don't just disappear from someone's life. But I did. I couldn't get away fast enough.

"I'm sorry, Mom. You must've been so confused. Scared. I'm sorry." It mattered little that she didn't move, didn't respond. She still had ears to hear.

"Look what Elena sent for us," Dane said, lifting up a basket.

I immediately smelled tortillas and onion and cheese. "Ooh," I moaned, rising to look inside the basket too. Foil-wrapped containers filled the basket, some still hot, some cold.

Dane waggled his eyebrows at me. "Want a picnic dinner?"

"Sounds fabulous." I went to the closet and pulled out a blanket, spreading it across the cold tile floor of Mother's room. "Smell that, Mother?" I called. "Elena's been at it again, cooking us a Christmas dinner. Remember the time we went to her house for carnitas and tamales on Christmas Eve?"

"Elena's been good to you, hasn't she?" Dane said, carefully setting out container after container.

"The best. I don't think we'd be here today if Elena hadn't been part of our lives. She always kept Mother and me rooted somehow. Helped us remember our foundations every time an earthquake pushed us off."

There were bowls of *queso fundido,* melted cheese with mushrooms, and *chile poblano* strips to put on the freshly made tortillas. There were four *tamales verdes de pollo,* chicken tamales with green sauce. There was a sweating, cold jar of sangría, fresh lime and orange wedges floating in a swirling current. A clay pot held *sopa de tortilla.* Elena had included small packages of avocado, cilantro, and sour cream to put on top of the warm soup. To finish off the meal, there was a small *flan blanco,* a prized recipe of Elena's that was really not flan in the traditional sense—it contained no egg yolks or milk—but did have flan's caramel topping and the delightful surprise of an airy, meringue-type filling.

With all this laid out before us, I felt as if I had been invited as the guest of honor at a surprise feast. Dane's stomach rumbled loudly, and we laughed together. He reached for my hand and prayed, "Father God, thank you for this incredible meal. For Doña Elena and all she has been to Charlotte and Krista, for her family, singing tonight in honor of you. Please bless this food and prepare our hearts for tomorrow morning, when we again encounter your Son. Amen."

"Amen," I said.

We dug into the tamales, the soup tureen built for two, and finally reached the grand prize of flan blanco. As I fed Dane the last bite, I glanced outside to see if it was snowing. It wasn't. But it felt as if it were. That was how perfect that Christmas Eve of Mother's last year was. Almost snowing. And I was happy, really happy for the first time I could remember.

There was no colder Christmas in New Mexico than the year that we buried both Oma and Opa. I insisted on visiting their graves on Christmas Day, wanting to grab some feeling of being close to them. Mother agreed, which surprised me. She hadn't gone to their grave sites since we'd buried them. It was Elena, always Elena, who took me to place flowers by their headstones.

But we stood out there, the cold Rio Grande wind whipping past us, our hair flying like angel wings about our faces. I made myself stand still and remember Oma bustling around the kitchen, making us dinner, and Opa gesturing toward himself,, inviting me to come and read.

"They loved you," Mother said, putting an arm around my shoulders.

I paused, letting the sound of "love" settle into my ears, appreciating the rare physical gesture from Mother. I dared to put an arm around her waist.

"They loved you, too."

"I know it." She bent then, took my hand in hers, and placed the bouquet of Christmas red roses by Oma's headstone. I did the same on Opa's. "They aren't here, Krista. Just their memories are with us now.

They are happier. Singing and laughing and feeling good. They'll be waiting for us. You know that, right? When we get to heaven, they'll be waiting for us. All will be forgiven, and we will laugh and dance and be happy, be really and truly happy."

She sounded so wistful, I shivered. It was almost like she wanted to be there right that instant. And yet, I had to admit that it sounded good. "You think it will be like that, Mother? Heaven will be that good?"

She looked at me then. "That good and even better."

Chapter Fourteen

December 25

I awakened the next morning as the sun spread its pastel Southwestern light across the arroyos and canyons and hills and mountains of the Rio Grande Valley. I glanced up, surprised to find myself still curled up in Dane's arms, a position in which we both had fallen asleep sometime around two o'clock. We never went to church, electing to stay with Mother instead, lighting candles along her window sill in the last candlelight vigil of her life.

I looked over at them, now extinguished. The labored breathing sounds from Mother's bed told me her struggle was not over. Stiffly, carefully, I pulled out of the once-comforting position, letting my left arm have its share of blood again. I rolled my neck and straightened my collar, then blinked hard, trying to gain focus.

Dane stirred and looked up at me as I rose. "Good morning."

"Merry Christmas," I said sleepily. "Guess it was good no one came in to see you lending such succor to a patient's family member."

"You're not just any patient's family member. Let 'em come in."

"Brave man," I teased.

"How's Charlotte?"

"Seems to be the same. I have a Christmas wish though."

"What is it?"

"Coffee. Hot. Tall. With cream."

"Just call me Santa," he said. He rose and tried to brush the wrinkles out of his shirt and slacks but to no avail.

"Looks like you slept in your clothes. What kind of man does that?"

He pulled me close, tracing my face with his index finger. "A man in love with a woman who insists on bedside vigils."

"Ah. That kind of man."

"Merry Christmas, Charlotte," he said, looking over at Mother. "I need a word from you sometime soon. I'd like to ask for your daughter's hand."

My heart started to pound fast. Was he serious? Or just teasing me? "You better be good, or she might turn you down for a better suitor," I said, trying to lighten the moment.

I moved to her bed and gazed down at her. Dane came over to stand beside me. "Merry Christmas, Mom," I whispered. I was tired for Mother, ready for her to be free, to go on. "She must be so exhausted."

"Yes," Dane said. He laid a hand on my shoulder, tucked a strand of hair behind my ear. "You ready? For her to go?"

"Yes."

"That's good. Do me a favor."

"What?"

"Tell her. Tell her it's all right to leave now. Sometimes...sometimes patients hold on, as if they're waiting for permission."

I let out an unladylike snort. "Mother never sought my permission. Ever."

He cocked his head and looked me in the eye. "Maybe she did. All the time. You just never looked at it that way." He let that sink in for a moment, then said, "Coffee. Cream. I'll be back." With a quick kiss on the cheek he was gone, and I turned my attention back to Mother. It was five o'clock. Every hour was such effort. Could she really be waiting for something from me?

I blew out my cheeks and looked at the plaster ceiling. "Give me the words, Father," I whispered.

I looked back to Mother and smiled, thinking back across the years. "Remember that Christmas when we got tacos at Juan's and went out to the gorge to watch the sunset? You called it a Christmas sunset. I'll never forget it. You and I sat there watching the sun sink between the mesas, and the sky was this amazing cast of persimmon and watermelon and mango. We watched as the last sliver of sun disappeared, and you looked over at me and smiled and ran a hand through my hair. And we just sat there for a minute. All quiet. Remember that, Mom?

"Or when we went to the homeless mission and served Christmas dinner to all those people? I was probably eleven or so. You didn't want to be home, missing Oma and Opa. I'll never forget what that was like, Mother. To know, to see people who had nowhere to go. I felt lucky that Christmas. It was like the first time I really understood all that I had."

I'd forgotten it over the years, all that I had. But I had understood and appreciated it once. I had been so lost, so buried in the anger and fear and frustration and guilt and sorrow and longing… My mind leapt to many other less pleasant Christmas memories, but I stubbornly returned to those I could look back on with a smile.

I reached out to trace Mother's cheekbone. "You didn't do all bad, Mom. You did a lot right. A lot right." My mind swept over the times in the dance studio when she smiled at my steps, nodded in satisfaction. Over times in church when she tickled my neck to keep me still when Pastor Muñoz's sermons got too long and I grew too squirmy. When she came into my room, thinking me asleep, and sat beside me, humming the old Spanish tunes she loved as if she wanted to imprint them on my memory. I had forgotten. So much. I had gotten so lost in what I didn't have, I'd forgotten what I had.

Mother struggled to take another breath, and I smiled sadly at her. "Mom, it's Christmas. You've made it to your last Christmas. Can you see him, Mom? Can you see Jesus? Is he a baby where you are? Or is he a man, opening his arms and welcoming you home?" I started crying now, tears running down my face, choking my words.

"Mom, you can go to him. I'm okay now. Really. I finally figured out that I love Dane. He loves me. You don't need to stay with me anymore, Mom. I have Dane. I have Elena. I have me now. I'm whole. You can go. Be free and breathe again. Please. I'll see you again. In heaven. And we'll say…all the words…we didn't say here." That last sentence really busted me; I could barely get out each word. "I'll hug you so tight…and I'll let you hug me. At last. I love you, Mom. Merry Christmas."

I reached for a tissue and then bent over to embrace my mother. When I straightened, a single tear rolled down the side of her face into her ear. It caught the light from the window, then faded.

I wiped it away. "I know, Mom," I whispered. "I know."

She was leaving. There were longer pauses between breaths. Dane had been right. She had been awaiting my permission somehow.

Taking a sip of water, I cleared my throat and leaned close to her, singing softly. "Truly He taught us to love one another; His law is love and His gospel is peace." The meaning of the words made me cry all the harder; I had to pause to try to continue. "Chains shall He break, for the slave is our brother, and in His name all oppression shall cease. Sweet hymns of joy in grateful chorus raise we…"

Dane entered, and the light in his face dimmed when he saw me standing over my mother, struggling to sing, tears streaming down my face. He set down the coffee mugs and wrapped his arm around me. "Let all within us…" he sang, picking up the hymn.

His presence pulled me together, and I shakily joined him, "praise His holy name. Christ is the Lord," we sang, my voice pathetically strained, but never had it sounded sweeter, more right to me. "Oh, praise His name forever! His pow'r and glory evermore proclaim! His pow'r and glory evermore proclaim."

The room felt supercharged, like the air during a lightning storm. My ears became full, as if underwater, and the hairs on my skin stood on end. "Do you feel that?" I whispered to Dane, my eyes on Mother. "He's here. He's coming for her."

Dane did not answer. He only squeezed my shoulder and held on tight.

Being present in that room that day took my breath away, like standing in a wind tunnel might. Or feeling the first wave of an explosion and living to tell about it. Yet it was gentle, comforting, warm from the inside out. I was never afraid. Just...overwhelmed by the Presence.

Mother took a deep breath, the deepest I'd heard since arriving in Taos again. It was as if she filled herself up with heaven and let herself drift from this world into the next.

I cried, but I was smiling, laughing through my tears in gratitude and gladness that Mother's strife was over. That she was free, free to bow at her Maker's feet and hover in the midst of his pow'r and glory and evermore proclaim with the angels all that he had done.

I took her hand. It was cold and still. "Good-bye, Mom," I said, through my tears. "Go with God."

Dane covered our hands with his. "*Vaya con Dios,* Charlotte."

We buried Mom three days later, and as I picked up a handful of the red New Mexican dirt that she had loved all of her days and tossed it on the coffin, the pastor recited the ancient rites, "Dust to dust…" I was glad she had died on Christmas Day. At Cimarron she had learned that Christmas could come every day, that each morning was a chance to embrace the Christ child again. Through her words in the book of carols she had taught me that.

The pastor spoke of a life well lived, of sorrows survived, of celebrations missed, but through it all a connection with the living God who saved. A Mexican trio played quietly in the background, first a mournful song that Mother had always loved, then a *despedimientos*, a traditional graveside hymn. It was profoundly moving to hear them play it, and a man sang the words to "Adiós, acompañamiento," which translated "Farewell, companions."

My ears heard Spanish, my mind English. "Adiós, acompañamiento, donde me estaban velando, a se llegó la hora y tiempo…encomienden mi alma a Dios, no me vayan a olvidar!" *Farewell, companions, where they watched over me, the hour and time have come…commend my soul to God, do not forget me!*

Once reserved for only the *hermanos* who inhabited such places as the adobe morada, the *penitente* brothers, who felt the remorse of sin to their very core, now the old hymns were sung by folklorists who wanted only to preserve a precious part of New Mexico's culture. I thought it appropriate that the words of godly men who had understood the far reaches of human depravity were now words for all people. How far I had sunk into my own web of self-preservation and blame laying. Not that I needed to whip myself in penance—I understood the power of grace and Jesus' sacrifice—it was just good to remember that we were all culpable, sinful, accountable. Dependent on mercy.

I looked around Mother's grave. We were a small group, mostly Elena's family and Cimarron staff and volunteers. A few old people were there too, holding on to canes and wool coats against an icy winter wind that blew off the Great Mountain to where the bones and flesh of my mother would lay forever. I allowed a humorless smile to spread across my lips, my tears long spent. It was apropos, this wind, over a body cold, the soul departed for warmer, more inviting places.

The pastor invited us to join him in an a cappella round of "Amazing Grace," and the Mexican trio added a wonderful harmony to the chorus that I would never forget, that I hoped would live in my memory until the day I would pass into eternity. It was so simple and beautiful, I longed to ask for one more verse.

Instead the last note held and disappeared on the wind, and with it, I felt as if the last piece of all that made up my mother swirled and swooped up to heaven.

Elena put on the funeral feast. We gathered for food and more food, then went into her small, enclosed yard for a dance. It honored Mother to end this day with dances that paid homage to her memory. The Mexican trio played one song after another. Those of us who remembered the centuries-old dance steps rose to dance and teach others who had not had Charlotte Mueller to guide their way. Dane and I led the group. First to the folk dance of *la varso-viana,* danced in three-quarter time, beginning all in a line in couples. We stepped into the second beat, feet raised, smiling more and more as we moved in the rhythm that Mother had so loved.

I led the way around the courtyard, the first of twenty dancers, some old, some young miming the crazy antics of the adults. And Dane was right there, as he had been all along. How blind I had been.

The trio began to play a traditional valse, and Dane led me with such aplomb that I got lost in the music, in his strong hands and his kind, loving eyes. We quickly moved into *el vase de los paños,* the handkerchief dance, which was performed with one man to two women. There were only nine of us who knew enough of it to take a stab at the complicated steps. I laughed and laughed when we got so confused that I ended up with a handkerchief wound around my back and my own arm wrapped around my neck.

We danced numerous polkas and eventually ended with the chote, or contra dance, that the Germans called a schottische. Mother always thought it a French interpretation of the Scottish two-step, not Spanish in origin at all, but she loved it nonetheless. As Dane and I faced each other, holding hands, and with the first beat headed to his right, I could almost hear Mother chanting, "right, left, right," then, "left, right, left." We proceeded into the waltz position and danced a polka step, and I smiled, remembering Mother, so proud in the corner of her studio as she watched Dane and me tour the room. Why had I forgotten such moments? Memories were like coins. Left in the rain, they faded, the original luster buried under mineral deposits. They needed to be kept safe, treasured, and admired.

"Your mother was a great dance teacher," Dane said, bending near my ear.

"Yes, she was," I said, leaning back in tempo. We finished the dance and then retreated to the side of the patio. It was late. It was time for me to pay the musicians and allow the weary families to take their exhausted children home. Though all seemed cheered by the dance, I knew that many would pay for it tomorrow if they didn't get the wee ones to bed.

I stood near the front door and thanked each person for coming, for helping me to say good-bye to Mother. Dane helped clean up the dishes in the kitchen. Elena stood beside me, her arm around my waist. When the last guest disappeared through the door, she smiled up at me. "Charlotte would have liked that."

"She would have. I wish we had done it before she was so ill."

"It is all right, dear one. In her mind she remembered the old days, the old dances. She remembered when she was young and thin and unwrinkled. She remembered when she loved and laughed."

I stared down at her, hoping she was right. "You think so?"

"I know so. Now send your young man home for his rest, and you get to bed yourself."

"Yes ma'am. And, Elena, thank you. Once again, for everything. You were the best of friends to my mother. And always to me."

"I always will be, my sweet."

"Gracias, Doña Elena. Gracias."

C H A P T E R F I F T E E N

December 29

I awakened the next morning in Elena's lovely guest room. Today I needed to clean out Mom's room so the Cimarron staff could move another patient in. There was something so final about it, beyond burying her, that I was reluctant to go. The storage unit would just have to wait awhile. It was enough to face this. And the headstone waiting for me at the granite yard.

I sat up and swung my legs out from under the down comforter, feeling the heated tiles beneath my feet. I padded into the bathroom and washed my face and brushed my teeth. Dane would come for me, I knew. He would be ready and waiting to see me through this last stage of saying good-bye to Mother. It comforted me to know that, but this morning I wanted a little time alone.

I brushed out my hair and pulled it into a knot behind my head, then returned to my room to put on a pair of jeans and a black turtleneck. The forecast had been for winter sun, but the cool wind off the mountains was to continue.

Elena was not home—off to the store I learned from the note she'd left—as if she knew I would want to get some air this morning. She had left me a pumpkin muffin and coffee in a thermos. "Thank you, God," I whispered, picking them both up, "for Elena. For Dane. You have been good to me."

I pulled on my cowboy boots, sitting by the door on the old banco, then my coat, and headed out to the far side of Elena's house, stooping to pet a wandering tabby cat. Then I took the path that led to the garden. My anxiety began to calm amid the exquisitely landscaped environment, even winter-dormant as it was. A tiny brook wound its way down the hill, under a miniature bridge, and out to a huge pond. A meticulously manicured gravel path wandered this way and that, lending itself perfectly to a meditative walk. Above, huge cottonwood trees spread their branches in a canopy that, come summer, would lend some shade. Now the bare branches let the hazy December sun warm my shoulders and scalp.

I took my muffin and meandered down the curvy walkway, pausing at fountains—now dry to avoid freezing during the coldest months. There was a kinetic sculpture that moved in the wind and other static designs of marble and tin and stone. Some were as short as two feet, some as high as nine. My path ended at a small pond, dug some fifteen years before.

I sat down on a stone bench and tucked my knees beneath the curve of my arms. The wind blew across the gray water, rustling through the brown, dried cattails and, beyond them, the winter-bare willows and young birch trees. My own private sanctuary.

I was reluctant to return to my sweet little cottage among the pines back in Colorado. It wasn't just Dane. It was something deeper. This place called to me, whispering in my ears of peace and promises of future joy. When I closed my eyes and raised my face to the sun, its rays seemed to penetrate my skin, filling me with light inside.

This feeling of tranquillity was new. Was it a passing phase? Or something that would last now that I'd let go of Mother, let go of the past? Was it because of the love I shared with Dane, my daring to embrace a future with him?

I need your strength to see all this through, Father. To see life through. I need you to show me which steps to take next.

For a long time I simply rested in his presence, relieved to know I was not alone in the decision before me, that I didn't have to carry my burdens by myself.

It came to me then, a whisper in my heart that became a shout. *Love is not without risk. But without love, there is little in life to live for.*

I knew then it just might work this time.

He discovered me in Mother's room, packing boxes of sweaters and the few clothes that remained in her possession, the books on the shelves, a few knickknacks… I was moving slowly, considering each piece and remembering, remembering things I hadn't thought of in years. I reached up and took down the glass ornaments I had hung from her window.

"Is this hard for you?" he asked softly, kissing me as he gently pulled me into his arms.

"Yes," I said with a slight nod. I rested in his embrace, staring out the window. "Sad. That I'd worked so hard for so long to forget the good."

Dane sat down on the edge of the bed and studied me. "I remember coming to your house when we were maybe nineteen. It was the first time I saw her really flip out. She was ranting about some lady who had stolen her sewing machine. Said she was going to call the police. She paced back and forth, hands on hips, but never picked up the phone."

"Oh yeah," I said, remembering too. "That was a really bad period. When she got so suspicious and paranoid. Life became one huge attempted assault for a while."

"It was that day that I really started to think about Alzheimer's," Dane said. "It was like a calling, seeing your mom that way. Knowing what she had been, what she had once been capable of. I knew I wanted to help people like her."

"See?" I asked wryly. "There's another thing Mother did right. Helped you figure out your life's work."

He turned me in his arms. "She did some things right with you. Look how you turned out."

"Yeah. Some." I looked into his eyes. "Dane, thank you, for taking such good care of Mother these last few years. I really would have gone insane trying to do it myself. And I doubt, I seriously doubt, I would've ever come to this place of peace with her. Without Cimarron. Without you. I really appreciate both you and your work."

He pulled away a little, eyes narrowing. "Why does this sound like a good-bye?"

I was silent for a moment, trying to find the words.

"Krista?"

"No, no, it isn't good-bye. I just want to make sure you know…that you know how important these last years have been. That you were there for Mother. When I wasn't. That you've always been there for me. All this time."

We stared at each other for a long, tender moment. He took my hands in his. "You sure you're not saying good-bye?"

He was as frightened as I, perhaps more so. I'd hurt him before, left him behind. And here he was, placing his life in my hands.

I smiled and stroked his face, feeling the strong cheekbones and stubble of the morning's beard growth beneath my palm. "Dane, I don't deserve you."

"Why do you say that?" he whispered, holding me steady in his gaze.

"I've been unkind. I've been abrupt. I've been unloving."

"Krista. Love." He waited until I dared to look him in the eye again. "I've always seen all you could be. You're like…like an incredible flower in germination, waiting for the right season to rise and bloom. Now is your season, Krista."

I smiled at his words. "Are you sure?"

"Kristabelle. While I think I've always known that we were to be together, this feeling inside me is new, alive. It's different now. I think it's God's way of telling me that this is the right time, the right season."

As he spoke, my heart swelled with peace and pleasure. He was right. God was blessing us. Showing us the way. *I'll trust you, Father. One more time.*

And maybe it would give me the courage to trust again and again and again.

Dane met me at the old cemetery on my way out of town. I wanted to say one last good-bye to Mother and to him.

They had installed the headstone the day before, and as I parked my car, it surprised me to see its smooth mauve surface glinting in the harsh winter sun. The dirt before it was fresh and slightly mounded, a natural contrast to its clean edges and chiseled font. Wordlessly, Dane opened my car door and offered his hand. We walked closer to the grave, then split up on either side.

I knelt at the top and to one side—as if afraid to step on Mother—and pulled my glove off to run my fingers over the elegant script. *Charlotte Elizabeth Mueller 1930–2002 Once lost. Now found.*

"I like it," Dane said, smiling into my eyes.

"Me, too."

"I had wondered what you would put on it."

"I did too. Once I worried I would not have anything to say.

Turns out I wanted the same on her headstone that I would want for my own."

Dane glanced down at the dirt and then back at me. "I'm glad, Krista. For you. That you've discovered what you need, what you want, what—"

"Who I love. What I love. You. God. Taos. It's coming together, Dane."

He rose and looked at me with an unspoken question in his eyes.

"I'm coming back, Dane," I promised. "I need to talk to my boss and work out a good transition, and then I'll come back. You and I can talk, figure out where we're going."

"We've talked. I know where I want us to go. The question is, do you?"

I dared to keep my eyes on his. "I do. You're the most perfect person in my life, other than Elena. And even more handsome."

He grinned and kissed me. "That's good to hear. You called St. John's?"

"Yep. The job offer still stands."

"Now you have to figure out if you want to take it."

"I love my school, my classes. It's tough to leave a job you love. And I've built up some years toward tenure..."

Dane took my hands. "It's gotta be right, Krista. It all feels on track for me. It's gotta feel the same to you."

"I understand. I want it to be right, Dane. I love you."

"You love me."

"I love you."

He beamed then. "Well, it's decided then."

I smiled shyly up at him. "Just give me a few weeks to go home and confirm what I know is in my heart."

"Okay then, go, go! Hurry up and get started so you can hurry up and come back to me."

His last hug and kiss stayed with me as I drove the roller-coaster hills toward Colorado. He had insisted that I take his sweater with me, I think more to remind me of him than from any real concern over my being cold. Again and again I reached for the olive cotton, pulling it to me as if I were hugging the man himself, inhaling his scent. How had I ever forgotten what he was like? How had I ever left him before? What I sought came to me before I passed the crosses on the hill in Carillo, before I passed through the old mining community of Walsenburg, before the mountains gave way to the raffia-colored prairies that extended all the way to Kansas, and I turned north toward the Springs.

I was missing him. In Taos.

I had rediscovered home. Forgiveness. Peace. Christmas.

And I couldn't wait to get back.

Dear Readers,

God's working on me in many ways, and for some reason this book didn't come easily. I hope it doesn't show in the outcome! I'm wrestling with what he wants me to do with my writing skills, where he's sending me. Right now, *God Encounter,* my prayer book that releases in December 2002, fills my heart and mind and calls me to the keyboard again and again. For more information on that, see the Web site www.GodEncounter.com.

Two things I need to set straight: My mother is a wonderful woman, and I was blessed to have her as my mentor, friend, and role model as I was growing up. I still appreciate her as such today and can't imagine the pain that women suffer when they cannot be close to their moms. I pray that each of you finds comfort in the arms of the Savior if you can't find it in the arms of your own mother. I also hope that this story encourages you to do everything you can to better understand your mother—or your daughter—and thereby come to a place of forgiveness and peace. Sometimes we're just wired differently, aren't we? Sometimes we just have to accept those differences and move forward as best we can.

Also, for those of you suffering through the trauma of Alzheimer's, I am writing this letter *to you* and sending along a special prayer of sustenance and encouragement *for you.* I know your road is long and harrowing at times. I had two grandparents who suffered from Alz, and it was painful to watch such wonderful, sharp people literally slip away. Know that the God of comfort and promise watches over you and holds you close through your pain.

Unfortunately, Cimarron is fictional, a combination of the best contemporary research I could find on alternative therapies in treating Alz patients. For more information on Alzheimer's, please call your local chapter of the Alzheimer's Association, or see their Web site at www.AlzheimersAssociation.com.

Every good thing,

Lisa Tawn Bergren

www.lisatawnbergren.com

OTHER BOOKS BY LISA TAWN BERGREN

The Bridge

THE FULL CIRCLE SERIES
Refuge
Torchlight
Pathways
Treasure
Chosen
Firestorm

NORTHERN LIGHTS SERIES
The Captain's Bride
Deep Harbor
Midnight Sun

NOVELLAS
"Until the Shadows Flee" in *Letters of the Heart*
"Tarnished Silver" in *Porch Swings & Picket Fences*

CHILDREN'S
God Gave Us You
God Gave Us Two